ITALIAN SECRETS / OUT OF SRI LANKA

JAN HOOK

BARJAN
BOOKS

I dedicate this book to my very dear, late husband Barry.

Two very different stories, in which all is not as it seems.

Italian Secrets

1

——

Lucy sat on the little terrace watching a solitary bee lazily hovering between the lavender flowers, landing every so often to gorge himself on the tasty nectar. How she loved the early mornings here.

They couldn't believe their luck when they found this ground-floor apartment – small, but perfectly formed, they decided. She had left him sleeping, resisting the urge to snuggle up and disturb him, to sit and enjoy these first sights and sounds of the day. She stretched out her legs, cradling her cup of coffee.

As she watched the bee her mind wandered, as it often did, and her best friend came into her thoughts. Friends since infant school, she had instinctively felt the need to protect Claire, from what she didn't always know, but as they grew older together the instinct never left her and when Claire had told her she thought Darren might be going to propose and she'd said to Lucy, "If he does you will be my chief bridesmaid, won't you Luce?" she'd shrieked her reply – whether in warning or anticipation, she wasn't sure.

Two months after inviting Lucy to be chief bridesmaid, Claire had turned up sobbing at Lucy's door, her blonde hair lank and her eyes ringed with dark shadows. Darren had, it seemed, got cold feet about any thoughts of a wedding and had said he really wasn't sure if he wanted to settle down. Between sobs, Claire eventually managed to tell Lucy the whole story. It was over. Darren had said he wanted a complete break!

"Why didn't you tell me before?" Lucy chided. "I sensed something wasn't right, but you didn't say! Oh, Clairabelle, I'm so sorry! Is it definitely over?"

Claire hiccupped. "All Darren said was that things in his life had changed and, although he still loved me, circumstances meant that our relationship had to end and he couldn't tell me any more!

"I asked him if there is someone else but he was adamant there isn't. I just couldn't tell you, Luce, I was too dazed by it all!"

Lucy's attention was caught by a Red Admiral butterfly as it vied with the bee for the lavender flowers, and her mind wandered on.

Two years ago, Lucy was on her way to a pretty Italian resort with Claire and two more of her friends, Dawn and Rosa.

"Come on, girls, I want to get to the airport in plenty of time. You know what it's like getting through customs at the moment!" Lucy chivvied.

Rosa rolled her eyes at the other two and muttered, "It's like being back at school!"

"Do you remember that far back then, Ro-Ro?" Dawn laughed.

"Cheeky! I'm not that much older than you!"

"Claire! Wake up love, are you getting in?" Lucy nudged her friend. Although outwardly she seemed to be getting her life back on track since Darren had left her heartbroken, there were times when her friends saw a few cracks in her outwardly bright demeanour. Claire snapped out of her reverie. "Sorry Luce, not awake yet. Who picked this early flight, anyway?"

Finally they were at the airport, through customs and on the plane. The flight made good time and a few hours later they were booked into their apartment and gathered on the huge balcony. They'd chosen this hotel because it meant that they were all together, but could have some personal space when they needed, or wanted it, and the balcony had enough loungers for all of them.

"Oh this is the life!" Rosa yawned as she stretched out on her lounger, sighing a deep contented sigh. "Did you think we'd ever get here?" she asked sleepily to any one of her friends who cared to reply.

Dawn shifted herself into a more comfortable position before replying, "When Mum was so poorly I didn't think I'd want to go this far away from her ever, but now that she's back to normal I'm sooo pleased to be here with all of you!"

Lucy rolled onto her tummy and looked over at Claire who was sitting up reading her book, lost in the story. She seemed to be slowly coming out of her depression but still wasn't as bright and bubbly as the old Claire had been. They all hoped she would gradually get back to her old self and tried to let her have her quiet moments when she seemed to need them.

"Good story?" Lucy asked.

Claire looked up and smiled. "Not bad, but I have to keep reading bits again as my eyes start closing!" She stifled a yawn.

"It's so relaxing here, isn't it? And I think we were all more than ready for this break. It's taken us such a long time to get it sorted and get here, hasn't it?" Lucy had barely got the words out when there came an ear-splitting scream.

"Where on earth did that come from?" said Rosa.

They all got up and peered over the edge of the balcony. "It sounded as though it came from that direction." Claire pointed towards a fairly busy part of the beach, "but sound gets distorted around the bay because it echoes."

"Look," Rosa said. "There seems to be a bit of a hubbub going on down there." She pointed to an area where a group of people were starting to gather. "I hope no-one's badly hurt."

2

Later, down in the restaurant, the girls were busily helping themselves from the buffet.

"I'm starving!" Rosa whispered to Lucy at her side.

"Well, you do surprise me!" Lucy joked.

Rosa gave her a playful punch. "Alright, so I get hungry!" They were giggling and playfully jostling each other, so didn't see the swarthy looking man standing over to the side of the restaurant watching Claire and Dawn, who had moved on to the pasta dishes – there were several tasty choices, but casarecce, with its mix of pasta twists, cherry tomatoes and spring onions, tossed in a simple dressing of olive oil, red wine vinegar and tabasco, was a particular favourite of Claire's. His dark eyes followed them for several seconds as they moved around the room, then he turned on his heel and slowly left the restaurant, speaking casually to the young girl on the desk as he passed.

When the girls were in the hotel bar later, deciding whether to hit the town this evening, or wait until tomorrow, after they'd done a bit of research to find the best places, they overheard snatches of a conversation from a British couple sitting at a nearby table. It was evident that they were discussing something that had happened on the beach that morning.

Try as they might, the girls could only make out the odd word or two. "Young girl… blonde… dead," was all they managed to hear, their eyes becoming wider as they heard each word. Rosa signalled to them all to drink up and as casually as they could, the group left the bar.

As soon as they were out of earshot, Rosa said, "Did you hear what they were saying? That scream we heard must have been to do with a young girl dying somehow. She may have got into trouble in the water. What a tragic thing to have happened!"

Back in their apartment, the girls pondered on what could have occurred and because they found it all rather sad decided to hit the town after all to shake off the sad feelings.

It was through one of Rosa's work colleagues that they had heard of this resort. One day she overheard him talking about one of his mates having a sister that worked for a company in Italy and because her and the other girls had been discussing a trip, she asked him later more about the resort. "I don't know that much about it but I'll ask me mate," he'd said.

Although the resort was not one of the more popular in this part of Italy, they had chosen it because it seemed to have a balance of what each of them wanted from a holiday. Good restaurants for Rosa – "I like my food and it's part of my holiday to enjoy good food," – opportunity for quiet times for Claire – "I don't want to be a drain on you girls but sometimes I just like to be quiet," which the other three knew and was the reason for choosing the apartment – some nightlife especially for Lucy and Dawn, but which the other two would also like and this resort had, they found, a couple of nightclubs that looked promising. One of the clubs was loud, throbbing with life and full of fun and laughter, the other was more sedate with slightly softer music and more seating, but still sounded full of laughter.

Tonight, as they all felt the need to have their spirits lifted, they would head for the louder of the two.

The swarthy guy that had been watching the girls in the hotel restaurant stood at the end of the bar sipping his drink, watching them dancing. Was it coincidence or had he followed them there? Lucy and Rosa were laughing at Claire and Dawn doing an impression of the girls from ABBA. Claire had drunk rather a lot. Lucy thought it was doing her good to let her hair down and said so to the other two.

"They enjoy the dance!"

The swarthy guy pulled his gaze away from the girls and nodded to the barman in agreement. "Si," he replied, put his empty glass on the bar, said "Grazie," and left.

The barman shrugged, removed the glass and went to serve customers further along.

Claire came out of her bedroom yawning and rubbing her eyes with one hand, holding her head with the other. "Oh why did you let me drink so much?" she asked the other three, who were reviving themselves with a coffee that Lucy had thoughtfully been down to the restaurant for, as they preferred it to the instant stuff provided.

"You insisted you were perfectly fine when we tried to slow you up," Rosa giggled. "There's a coffee there for you, Lucy got them. Might only be lukewarm now but get it down you anyway, you look as though you need it!"

They just about got down to the restaurant before breakfast service finished, although none of them had much of an appetite, not even Rosa. Lucy, who seemed to have taken on the role of mother hen, said they all ought to eat something.

They discussed plans for the day. Lucy wanted to wander up to the old part of town to investigate the different architecture, a passion of hers. Dawn said she would go too, not that she had any particular interest in architecture, but she wanted to see what shops there were in that part of town – retail therapy was her passion.

Rosa, being the food expert and self-appointed restaurant guide, said she would have a wander and see where would be a good place for them to have their evening meal, meaning she might just have to try out a few of their snacks! Claire said that she might read by the pool for a while and then perhaps take a stroll along the beach.

After eating some cereal and a croissant and drinking one more sobering cup of coffee, they all agreed to meet up in the foyer at about 1pm to have a leisurely lunch in the hotel restaurant.

"Sure you'll be okay here?" Lucy asked, putting an arm around Claire's shoulder.

"I'll be fine, Luce, honestly. I haven't been out on the raz for a while, I need today to recover! Not used to it like you three!"

"Okay, if you're sure, enjoy your quiet time and we'll tell you all about our discoveries over lunch."

"Yes really, I'm sure. Go and enjoy your exploring!"

3

As predicted, Rosa stopped off in a couple of the restaurants and sampled the coffee and the odd pastry, thrilled when she found one she knew everyone would love. Loads of character, plenty of choices to suit all of their different tastes, not too upmarket and with just the right amount of charm. While she sat outside under the shade of a parasol at one of the tables, she took her notepad from her bag and made a note of the name of the restaurant and the street. It wasn't all that far from the hotel so really was ideal.

Lucy was enthralled with the different styles of architecture as she gazed up at the facade of yet another wonderfully designed building. She had left Dawn in retail heaven! They had happened upon a quirky boutique in a tiny side street. Seeing that Dawn would happily browse her way through everything in there for quite some time, they agreed Lucy would return in about 45 minutes.

She managed to find the boutique again and sure enough

Dawn was carrying a bag. "Oh Luce! This is such a brilliant little shop!"

Lucy and Dawn meandered their way back to the hotel and bumped into Rosa doing the same.

"Have you both had a good wander?" she asked.

"Oh we found this gorgeous little boutique! Look what I bought!" Dawn said excitedly, pulling from the bag a scrap of material.

"Oh that's lovely!" Rosa exclaimed. "Very unusual design on it, so pretty! What about you, Luce?"

"Oh there are some incredibly beautiful buildings in the town, so diverse in design, the detail on some of them is so intricate," Lucy enthused. "How did your restaurant reccie go?"

"Well, I have found us the most perfect restaurant for this evening! It is just so us!"

They chatted on about their respective passions until they got back to the hotel and headed for the foyer. "Let's find Claire and get some lunch," Rosa said when they arrived.

"She must be up in the apartment. I'll go and fetch her," Lucy said. "You two get the drinks in."

Rosa and Dawn were sipping their wine when Rosa spotted Lucy. "Lucy looks worried about something," she said. "Perhaps something's wrong with Claire. She isn't with her." They went over to Lucy. "What's wrong, Luce? Where's Claire?"

Lucy shook her head with a worried frown. "She's not in the apartment. I checked in her room and she's not there. It's not like Claire to go anywhere without saying anything, is it?"

"No it isn't, but didn't she say she was going to read by the pool?" asked Rosa. "I bet she's fallen asleep out there."

By the time they had looked everywhere they could think that Claire might be, all three were starting to feel anxious.

"I'm probably being dramatic," Lucy said, "but her room looked quite messy, which isn't like Claire, is it?"

"What about the beach?" Rosa asked. "She did say she might have a stroll. Perhaps she stayed down there and lost track of time."

The part of the beach the three of them decided she would probably explore was pretty crowded, but they worked their way along the stretch and it was evident that Claire was not anywhere to be seen. Lucy tried ringing Claire but it went through to voicemail. She left her a message.

Clairabelle, where are you? We're all back in the hotel now and can't find you. Can you ring back or text, we're getting a bit worried.

The manager of the complex was a very smart man, in his mid forties. Although he privately thought the girls were overreacting, he didn't want any complaints about his efficiency, it was his first year in this hotel! After the incident with the girl on the beach, he erred on the side of caution and said he would make enquiries among the staff.

"We've got to do something," Dawn said, after leaving his office. "We can't just wait about not knowing." After a moment, she added, "Why don't we ask around the other guests and see if they saw anything? I've got a photo of Claire on my phone from earlier today we can show people."

"Good idea! Come on, let's start in the restaurant." Rosa thought she would just grab a piece of bread or something as they passed through. She was feeling decidedly hungry now!

Apart from a couple of people they found by the pool, who said they had noticed Claire reading a book there some time ago, nobody could recall seeing her.

The girls were getting more anxious by the minute. "Let's try down on the beach," Rosa said.

Their spirits dropped when they saw the amount of people

had grown since they had been down before. "Bloody hell, where do we start?" Lucy said, a catch in her voice.

Rosa linked her arm through Lucy's. "Come on Luce, once we get started it'll be fine."

A lot of the holidaymakers were Italian but through broken language and with gestures of pointing to the photo, pointing to the person, then their eyes and back to the photo, people got the gist of what they were asking. A few also remembered Claire by the pool but nobody seemed to have seen her since then. By the time they had more or less asked everyone they could, they were feeling very downhearted.

"Right," said Rosa, trying to sound more positive than she felt. "I know the manager said he'd make enquiries but shall we work our way round all the staff in the hotel as well?"

They started with the bar staff, although they strongly doubted Claire would have come to the bar alone, it wasn't her style. As suspected, nobody recalled seeing her. They were getting more and more downhearted as they worked their way through as many staff members as they could find.

Dawn saw the young lad who had taken their luggage up to their apartment just coming out of the lift and went over to him. He could speak very good English. "Have you seen our friend since this morning?" She pointed to the photo on her phone.

"Yes, I saw this lady come out of lift with a man. She didn't smile at me. She has nice smile, I smile at her but she didn't smile back!"

Dawn called out to the others to come over and explained to them what the lad had said.

"What did the man look like? Which way did they go? Was she okay?" Lucy shot quick-fire questions at the boy.

"Luce, you're frightening the poor lad!" Rosa put her hand on Lucy's arm and turned to the boy. "It's okay, we're just trying to find our friend. Can you remember anything more about when you saw them?" she asked gently.

His face relaxed a little. He thought for a while, before saying, "I not see the man before. I don't know who he is, they went out to the strada. Sorry, I have seen no more." He shrugged apologetically.

"Thank you, you have been very helpful," Dawn said, touching his arm. She searched in her handbag for her purse.

"No senora, I like you help."

4

The officer at the polizia listened patiently but had the attitude that Claire had simply found a guy and gone off out with him. Seeing that so many times before, he was convinced that's what had happened, although he did note everything down before asking them to contact him if she hadn't returned by the morning and to let him know if she did return. He suggested the girls returned to the hotel in case Claire came back.

The girls went into the hotel restaurant early – Rosa's choice of restaurant not something they would explore that day, of course – although none of them really felt hungry, not even Rosa.

"I know the police think we're making a lot of fuss about nothing but I can't just wait here and do nothing," Lucy said. "You all know as well as I do that there is no way Claire would willingly just go off with some man without saying something to us, if at all!"

"But what can we do?" Dawn asked.

They discussed it further and agreed that all they could do

was to keep making a nuisance of themselves at the police station.

"At least it will keep Claire in their minds," Rosa said.

They decided to have a quick bite and then go back to the police station. Without much appetite, they picked about at a few bits of salad, had a quick drink and off they went.

The officer they had seen before wasn't there so they had to explain to another one, a handsome young chap. Lucy caught his eye just as he looked up and was surprised to feel a frisson of pleasure, even making her blush. He held her glance for a moment before continuing to listen. He checked the log that his colleague had noted, listened intently after they, between his grasp of English and their bits of Italian, had explained every detail, nodding when he fully understood and asking for more explanation when he didn't, making more notes all the while they spoke. Finally he put his pen down and said he would start by making enquiries from the locals that he knew and who would know if anyone different had been around the hotel. He explained that there were one or two who hung around the hotel entrance hoping to earn a few euros acting as tour guides. Everyone knew it wasn't legal but a blind eye was turned. Dawn said to the others that she remembered seeing a young girl approaching one of the guests who had waved her away and she hadn't thought any more of it.

It was agreed that they would, as he suggested, return to the hotel and stay in the bar should the young officer either have any information or need to speak to them again. He came round from behind his partition and held the door open for them to leave. Lucy's arm brushed his as she went past and again she felt that frisson! All three of them felt some relief that at least he was not fobbing them off as they felt the other older man had done.

They had been in the bar for a couple of hours, all agreeing that, after a first much needed hit of alcohol, they would stick to either spritzers or soft drinks just in case the polizia came, when the young officer came to find them. They all rushed at him and asked for news at once.

He put his hands up in a defensive action. "I 'ave little bit news," he said, holding his thumb and forefinger a little apart, and proceeded to explain that one of the young people he had asked had observed a man they hadn't seen before and who didn't seem to be a guest, come out of the hotel a couple of times. The officer said that he had just checked with the barman and he remembered a man of that description the night before. He indicated that it could well be as his colleague had suggested that she had met someone in the hotel and just gone out for the evening. All three of them knew full well that it just wasn't what Claire would do, but didn't labour the point. He was obviously going above the call of duty as it was.

"Thank you for telling us," Lucy said and again their eyes met. 'Whatever is wrong with me?' Lucy scolded herself. 'It must be the worry making me feel things that aren't there.'

At the policeman's suggestion they went back to their apartment to spend the rest of the evening there, with his promise that they would be kept informed of any news.

"E you tell us se lei come per fav... pleeze?" he asked.

"Oh God I feel exhausted!" Dawn said as she flopped down on the sofa a little later.

"It's the worry, I feel the same," Rosa agreed.

"My mind hasn't stopped whirring, imagining all sorts of

horrible scenes," Lucy said tearily. Dawn and Rosa went to her. They hugged each other tightly, all weeping. Dawn didn't even notice Rosa's tears were making her lovely new top all wet.

Suddenly Lucy's phone buzzed.

Hi Lou Lou, sooo sorry to worry you. Am ok, will xplain when back xx

"What does that mean?" Lucy asked. "It's so not Claire, is it?"

Lucy sent back a reply.

Are you sure you're ok?

Really am fine. Can't msg more now XXX came Claire's response.

It was seven in the morning when Lucy, always a light sleeper but even more so as she worried about Claire, snapped her eyes open when she heard the apartment door unlock. Dawn came out of her bedroom, running her fingers through her hair and hastily tying a belt round her dressing gown, closely followed by Rosa, yawning, rubbing her eyes and shaking her head to wake herself up.

When Lucy got to the door, she couldn't believe her eyes. "I'm sorry, I didn't want to disturb you!" Claire said, grabbing Lucy, and they just clung to each other, both with tears streaming down their faces.

Dawn and Rosa rushed to them, taking their turn with hugs. Lucy shakily grabbed some tissues and involuntarily plumped down onto the sofa. Dawn and Rosa released their hold on Claire and all three girls started talking at once.

"What happened?"

"Where did you go?"

"Are you alright?"

"Are you hurt?"

Lucy hugged Claire again. Rosa was making coffee for them all, the instant stuff not seeming quite so bad, and Dawn was busily getting mugs ready, Claire waiting until they were all together before she told them anything.

"We've been so worried," Lucy said, near to tears.

"I know you have and I'm so very sorry to have put you through all that," Claire sniffed.

Once all the girls were settled with coffee in hand, Rosa remembered a box of chocolates she had bought as a present and decided it would be better used now, so opened the chocolates and put them on the coffee table. Then they were all poised, ready to hear what Claire had to say.

"I don't really know where to start," she said softly.

"Why don't you start from where we left you downstairs," Lucy said gently.

"Right, well I nipped up here to get my book to have a read by the pool, but couldn't remember where I'd last had it, hunted high and low in my room then remembered I'd read it in here and found it down the side of the sofa," Claire said, waving her arm to indicate the lounge where they were all sitting. "So I grabbed it and went down to the pool. I hadn't been down there long when I remembered that I'd gone straight from here and left my room upside down after looking for the book and you know what I'm like?" she said, they all nodded in agreement, "I couldn't concentrate on my book until I'd come back to straighten it up."

The other three smiled knowingly. Anyone else would have said, 'Oh sod it, I'll do it when I go back up'!

"As I reached our apartment, a man came up to me and asked, 'Are you Claire?' When I said I was, he said 'I need you to come with me.' I asked him who he was and why I should go with him, edging towards our door to see if I could get in before he got too close."

"Oh my God Claire, you must have been so scared!" Dawn exclaimed.

"I was. But then he said, 'don't be afraid, I'm not here to harm you. Darren has asked me to get you'!"

"DARREN!" all three girls shouted at once.

"He gave me a letter from Darren," Claire continued. "I didn't know what to do as it was definitely Darren's writing and all he said was that he needed me to go with the man and he would explain when I got there."

Rosa gasped. "But he could have been anyone tricking you into thinking it was an innocent letter from Darren, could have trapped Darren and forced him into writing that note – he didn't, did he? Sorry girls, but it's all so odd!"

"I really didn't know what to think. It was all a shock and happened so quickly I couldn't think straight, then I tried to delay him, saying that I wanted to leave you a note but he said there was no time and rushed me off, firmly, but not roughly, then we got into a blacked-out car and drove off. I must admit, I was pretty scared then!"

Claire paused to have a long gulp of her coffee before continuing, "Eventually we got to a house that stood all alone at the end of a very long drive and before we got out of the car, he made me hand over my phone!" All three of the other girls sat agape with wide eyes, waiting expectantly for what Claire was going to say next.

"He kept telling me not to be afraid and assuring me that I wouldn't be hurt and took me into the house and showed me into a room, pointed to a door and told me that was a bathroom. There was a bed, an armchair and a small table with a chair in the room. Then he left and when he closed the door, I heard him turn a key!"

"OMG Claire, you must have been terrified!" Lucy said.

"I was! And I'm so, so sorry you were all so worried. I knew you would be, of course!"

"Go on Claire, tell us what happened next," prompted Dawn.

5

"I heard the key turn in the lock and couldn't believe my eyes when Darren came in!"

"What? Darren was there?" Dawn and Rosa both exclaimed at once, while Lucy choked on her coffee.

"Yes, Darren, I couldn't believe what I was seeing! I was so shocked I couldn't speak! Then Darren came to me and went to put his arm round me and I backed away. Surely he didn't think he could just pick up where we left off, for goodness' sake?! I had so many thoughts whirring around in my head. Why was he here? How did he know I was in Italy? Why did he bring me here? I was so confused!"

"The cheek of the man after what he did! I can't imagine what you were going through," Lucy said indignantly.

Claire took another sip of her coffee and helped herself to a chocolate, putting her hand up to the girls for them to give her a minute. "It's not what you think," she said when she'd swallowed the chocolate.

"Well tell us then, Claire!" Rosa said impatiently.

"Darren said," Claire continued, "that he was so sorry for

all the cloak-and-dagger stuff but it was essential that nobody saw us together, or that I contact you while I was with him, but I kept telling him that you would all be so worried so, eventually, he let me send that text."

"Oh my God Claire, this is like something out of a mystery novel. Can you put us out of our misery a bit quicker!" begged Dawn.

"Weeell, when Darren and I started seeing each other, he was actually using a false identity for his work, which he still can't tell me about."

All three of the girls looked shocked and said simultaneously, "Is he a spy or something?"

"I really don't know, he couldn't tell me and I was just really there to make it look a normal life."

"He used you?!" Lucy loudly demanded.

"To start with, yes, I was just part of the 'act' but Darren said as our romance got more serious he really fell in love with me and that wasn't part of the plan, he said he let his feelings get in the way of the part he was playing and knew that he shouldn't have let it get as serious as it did. Eventually he had to make what he said was the hardest decision he's ever had to make and broke up with me because he knew our relationship might put me in danger. Couldn't tell me why, nor did he want to carry on a charade. He said it wasn't fair to me. He would rather let me think he was a bastard and get on with my life. However, it ate at him so much that he couldn't let me go on thinking that he just didn't want me without letting me know the real reason."

"So is he no longer doing whatever he was doing, then?" asked Dawn.

"No! He still is, which is the reason for all the secrecy. I have no idea where I was taken, or who the man was that took me, have no idea who Darren really is, or where he has gone now, if or when I shall ever see him again, he just wanted to tell me he loves me, that he doesn't expect me to put my life on hold, but if I am still unattached when, and if, he can be free he will find me!" Claire wiped the tears from her eyes.

"Wow!" Lucy said. "So how—"

Claire had another slurp of her coffee, blew her nose and dabbed her eyes. Lucy put her arm around her. "Oh Clairabelle, I'm so sorry we're giving you the third degree. It's obviously been a pretty traumatic and emotional experience. Get your breath back, do you want to go and have a shower? Or a soak in the bath might be better to unwind a bit before you carry on?"

"Yes I will, if you girls don't mind. I'm feeling a bit shaky. Probably all hit me now."

The three girls fussed round her. Rosa got her some towels, Dawn ran the bath and put some of her expensive bubbles in while Lucy led her in to find some pjs and a fluffy dressing gown.

While Claire was in the bath, the other girls whispered amongst themselves.

"I can't believe this," Lucy said. "It doesn't seem real, does it?"

The other two shook their heads. "It's like something you'd see in a movie!" Rosa whispered back.

Dawn said, "Poor Claire, what a scary time she's had and how awful to be left with all that uncertainty!"

"Fancy Darren, or whatever his real name is, doing something undercover!" Rosa exclaimed.

Lucy sighed. "It's good for Claire in one way to know that he didn't just dump her, but how can she get on with life with that uncertainty hanging over her? We all know how much Darren meant to her, well, means to her I guess now, and I know Claire, she'll keep hanging on now just in case!"

Claire had enjoyed her soak in the bath, had gathered herself a little, but was still totally confused by all the events over the last couple of days and overhearing what Lucy had just said only made her more confused. She took a deep breath and re-joined her friends.

"Ah here she is!" Lucy exclaimed. "Feeling a bit better?"

"Yes, thanks Luce, not quite so shaky, but I think it'll take me a while to process it all, to be honest! I'm so sorry I've ruined the holiday for you all!"

"Oh Claire, stop keep saying sorry! I can't deny we were worried, of course we were, but now we know that no harm came to you, that's all forgotten, isn't it girls?" Dawn said, squeezing Claire's arm.

The others nodded in agreement. "Of course it is!" Lucy said.

They carried on chatting, Claire explaining that the man who had taken her to Darren had afterwards driven her by some back roads, pulled up at the rear of the hotel and let her walk round to the front, watching her all the time until she was inside the hotel, no doubt under instruction from Darren.

Lucy thought of the helpful young policeman. "We have to inform the police Claire's back safe and sound."

"Police?" Claire exclaimed. "Did you call the police? Oh I've caused so much trouble and worry, haven't I? I'm so sorry!"

Ever practical, Rosa turned to Claire. "Claire darling, you didn't cause any trouble, you had no choice in the matter, but of course we were worried and of course we told the police, but don't fret about it, we'll let them know everything's okay now."

"But they'll ask questions won't they and I can't implicate Darren in any way, can I?" Claire said worriedly.

"Oh the bloody man has caused us a problem, hasn't he?" Dawn exploded, immediately regretting her outburst upon seeing the tears well up in Claire's eyes, not to mention the glare Lucy gave her. "Oh Claire I'm so sorry, I think it's all the trauma making me ratty!" she said, as she gave Claire a hug.

Claire explained that Darren had actually said that if any questions were asked she was to say that an old friend, who was coincidently also on holiday there, had found out where she was staying and had sorted out what she thought would be a wonderful surprise for her and had whisked her away.

At the police station, Lucy was unaccountably disappointed to find that 'her' police officer wasn't on duty. They explained all to the duty officer, who they had seen in the first place, without, of course, any mention of Darren. He made a brief note and with a kind of 'I told you so' attitude, he was satisfied with their explanation and was happy to write off the incident as a typical tourists' escapade! The girls apologised for wasting their time and said their goodbyes. The officer thought they were some of the nicer tourists he'd come upon. He got to see all sorts during the tourist season, even in their little resort!

6

David Eastman was a bright lad who loved detective stories and infuriated his father by forever stating he was going to be a detective.

"You need to concentrate on your studies instead of living in that dream world," his father would reply.

"It's not a dream world dad and even if it was it's my dream, yours is being an accountant!"

Despite these arguments, David did add accountancy to his study list and, in actual fact, excelled at maths, seemed to have a natural ability to understand accountancy and, even though he never appeared to his parents to be studying all that hard, became a grade A student.

David was grateful to his father to have instigated his inclusion of accountancy in his studies as when an undercover detective was required to infiltrate a company belonging to a large conglomerate which was suspected of money laundering, he was considered suitable for the job. And so his 'other life' began...

David became Darren Evans, was installed in an

apartment, was given every necessary document in his new name, told his parents he was going abroad on an assignment and might not be in contact much and invented a whole new persona to enable him to slide into the new life. It wasn't long before he managed to obtain a post in the accounts department of the company, a perfect place for him to unobtrusively investigate. He played his part well, became 'one of the lads', joining the other guys, when invited, on different nights out, carefully finding excuses to avoid areas where he might be recognised. It was on one such outing that he was drawn to a very pretty girl with the most stunning blue eyes. She was very quiet and unassuming and gave him a shy smile when he caught her eye.

David found himself swept along in the romance, constantly telling himself that he shouldn't let it get serious as he was not who he was telling her he was, but he was so smitten, he couldn't help himself. He was in love!

7

Giorgio de Luca, a plain clothes detective from Italy, had been flown over to make contact with 'Darren Evans' when the money trail had led to Italy. The two men instantly got on well together. Darren made sure he didn't include Claire in anything that involved work, but he was finding it increasingly difficult. Although he didn't tell Giorgio anything about Claire he did confide in him about the situation and Giorgio agreed that, not only was it likely to compromise the assignment but could, as David feared, possibly involve Claire in a certain amount of danger and so it was that David did one of the hardest things he'd ever had to do in his life and told the girl he loved with all his heart that he wasn't ready to commit to her. It broke his heart to see how distraught she was and he felt like the lowest weasel going! Though he didn't regret meeting Claire and finding that love, he bitterly regretted letting it turn out the way it did.

David was good at his job, both as a detective and in his undercover profession, so when the trail led to Italy, he deftly engineered a reason within his accountancy remit to go over to 'expand the business opportunities', hence the legitimate meeting of Giorgio. It also meant that he would distance himself from Claire for a while.

Darren couldn't believe it when a colleague, who he had asked to keep an eye on Claire, had found out she was to go on holiday to Italy with some girlfriends and when he found out that the resort was in an area not too far from the town in which he was based, he couldn't let the opportunity go.

After Darren had explained as best he could, he gently took her hands and pulled her to her feet. He tilted her chin and softly kissed her trembling mouth. As Claire leaned into him, he wrapped his arms around her and his kisses became more urgent. Claire felt the familiar butterflies. Heart thumping, she gave in to her feelings and returned his passionate kisses.

"Oh Claire, I've missed you!" he breathed into her hair. He lifted his head and wiped away the tear that was rolling down Claire's cheek.

"I thought I'd never see you again. I love you so much!" Claire started to sob as it all became too much.

"You will never know what a bastard I felt, doing what I did. I came very close to telling you everything, but I couldn't and still can't, not just because of what I have to do but because if you don't know you won't be in danger."

Darren looked intently at Claire. She knew that fire in his eyes and felt the familiar tingle run up her spine. He walked slowly towards her and tenderly touched her face. She leaned into him, raising her mouth to his. He saw the heat in her eyes and led her towards the bed – and stopped.

"What's wrong?" she asked.

"I want you so much, but that isn't why I brought you here. I just wanted you to know how much I love you. I don't want to start something now that I don't know when, or even if, we can finish."

Claire sat down on the bed and was suddenly consumed by an emotion she very rarely felt. She started yelling at him. "You led me into thinking we were going to get married, you dumped me, you had some stranger bring me here, ruining the start of my holiday, you let me think we were going to make love just now and now you tell me that you love me but I might never see you again!" she ended with a sob.

Darren had never seen Claire in a temper before, never seen that flare in her eyes. She was always so mild mannered and gentle, even when he broke up with her. In fact, he'd have felt better if she had lost her temper. The quiet hurt in her eyes was much worse and had haunted him ever since. He sat down next to her and put his arm round her. At first she shrugged it off but as he tightened his grip she laid her head on his shoulder and sobbed once again. He lifted her face and kissed her tears. She pulled at his shirt, he lifted her top, groaned into her cleavage, and removing her bra he found her nipple. She threw herself back on the bed with a moan, pulling him down on her, their kisses urgent and passionate. She didn't care if they had just this time, she wanted him, he was unable to stop, his need greater than any reasoning!

"You could have really blown our cover and all those months of work would have gone down the drain!" said Giorgio, pacing up and down.

"I wouldn't have risked that, Gio, it was all safe, you know it was, you made sure of it!"

"I know, but I didn't like it and God help us both if the powers that be were to ever find out how you, we, compromised the job!"

"Well, it's done and I'm happy that I've seen Claire and

explained, although she knows nothing about any of it and has no way of doing so, I made sure of that!"

"Okay, we'll leave it there. Anyway, we'd better get back to the job in hand. I've found out that the girl that was washed up on the beach was the girlfriend of an assistant to one of the contabiles and guess what?"

"What?" Darren asked irritably.

"My source found out that during routine questioning of her friends it transpired that one of them works for that pharmaceutical company you traced!"

Darren was pretty sure the source of the money being laundered was the trafficking of cocaine and he and Giorgio were getting near to exposing the people involved. Darren had taken his time to gradually infiltrate the relevant accounts, but had to be careful to avoid any suspicion, so it was a long drawn-out process. This lead was definitely a step forward, as they knew that someone in that pharmaceutical company was involved.

"Could your source get you the name of that friend, Gio?"

"I don't know, I'll see what I can do."

"If you could find out who she is, can you try and get to speak to her somehow and see if you can find out anything?" Darren prodded. "In the meantime, I've got a chance of working in the chief accountant's office."

"Fantastica! Careful, though. We don't want to blow it now. I'd better get back to Gabriella, she wasn't happy about me spending most of my day off helping you 'look at a boat'! My life wouldn't have been worth living if she'd seen me with Claire, you owe me big time!"

"I won't forget it, Gio."

8

Luigi Marino was, as a lot of young Italian men are, a handsome young man. His parents, particularly his father, thought that he was far too soft natured to be a policeman, but he was very good at his job. Of course during the tourist season he met many young women and, he had to admit, he did have a few dalliances with some, nothing serious, he knew they just wanted a light-hearted holiday romance and, if he took to a girl, he happily enjoyed the romance.

When the English girls came to the station looking for their friend, he was struck by one of them in particular. There was something about her eyes with the little flecks of green in them and her velvety hair definitely needed fingers running through it. He was disappointed that they had come to say they had found their friend on his day off. Still, he knew where they were staying and vowed to find some excuse to 'bump into them' – well, her really!

All Claire wanted to do was to shut herself in her room and try to make sense of everything. Her mind, not to mention her heart, was in turmoil! But she knew what she had put the girls through and already felt as though she had ruined the start of their holiday, so what she said was, "Oh yes! We've still got to see this treasure you've found for us, Rosa, haven't we?"

Lucy mouthed to her behind Rosa's back, "Are you sure?" privately thinking that it was probably the last thing Claire wanted to do, but knew that Rosa was just trying to give Claire a boost. Claire gave Lucy an almost imperceptible nod.

Claire resolved to try to get into the spirit of things for the sake of her friends, although she had to admit she found it very hard. Of course, the girls were aware that it would be and for a day or two all of them were tiptoeing around each other.

"Do you feel like a beach morning?" one would ask. "Shall we just sit by the pool this afternoon?" asked another. "Anyone fancy an explore?"

In the end, it was Rosa who sorted out the 'problem'.

When they were all sitting in the restaurant Rosa had found ("Brilliant choice, Rosa!" they'd all agreed) having a leisurely lunch, she took a sip of her wine before saying, "Look girls, I think we're all trying too hard not to push, or upset you, Claire." She held her hand up as Claire went to speak. "And you are trying to join in a holiday spirit that you really don't feel. How about this for a suggestion? You, Claire, do what you feel comfortable with. If you want to join in with whatever we all, or one of us, decides to do then that will be great. If you just feel like dossing in your room all day stuffing consolatory chocolates, then that's what you do. As for us three, we're all here to enjoy ourselves in whatever way suits us so can we just say, 'I think I'm going to spend the day on the beach' or whatever takes our fancy, leaving it to be taken as said that if anyone wants to join in they will?"

Rosa slumped against the back of her chair, let out a huge breath and took a big swig of her wine. She'd dreaded making that speech but felt it needed to be done.

'Good old Rosa,' thought Lucy. 'She's absolutely right, as she normally is!' She'd glanced at Claire and saw her mouth twitch at the sides with the start of a smile when Rosa mentioned stuffing chocolates! All three girls were relieved that the pressure had been lifted. Claire got up and gave Rosa a hug, whispering, "Thank you!" in her ear and Dawn and Lucy reached across the table and squeezed her hands.

The next day, Claire had decided to sit by the pool with a book, Rosa and Dawn were browsing in the town, each looking for family presents to take home and Lucy had fancied having some time on the beach. She had enjoyed a good swim and was just about to lay on her towel to dry off, when a shadow fell upon her. She looked up to see her handsome policeman, Luigi, standing there. "Oh hello!" she said in a bit of a fluster and was pleased that she was wet from the sea as it, hopefully, hid the red flush she knew was rising up her neck!

"Sono qui per fare qualche domanda, ti ho riconosciuto e sono venuto a salutarti," he said by way of explanation then, seeing her frown, he tried his English, at which, gradually by chatting to tourists, not to mention young women, he was slowly getting more adept. "I am 'ere to ask... persones questions... I 'ave see you and vuole to say ciao." When he'd finished, he puffed his cheeks out with the effort.

Lucy wondered if his questions were anything to do with

the death of the young woman that they had heard about on their first day but resisted the urge to ask. It was difficult enough to make ordinary conversation. They 'chatted' a little, as best they could, until, finally, Luigi had to get on with what he was there for. "I 'appy to see you," he said, before leaving.

"Errmm... sono Felice di... see you too!" was all Lucy could manage, but he understood, grinned his charming grin, touched his hat, said "Ciao" and left.

When the girls met up in the evening, she told the others about her meeting.

"So did he ask you on a date then?" Dawn asked.

"Noo of course not!" was Lucy's indignant reply. "We were just chatting, well as best we could with my poor Italian and his pigeon English!" she chuckled.

"You'd have liked him to though, wouldn't you?" Dawn winked at her.

"He is a bit cute I have to admit, but I don't go in for holiday romances, you know that."

On their last night, as they didn't have an early flight the next day, they got dressed up in their glad rags to hit the town.

"Wow Luce, you look stunning!" Rosa gushed when Lucy came out of her room dressed in a calf-length, deep yellow figure-hugging dress, which, though it showed off her curvy figure, still managed to look sophisticated and was a great colour to show off her tanned arms and dark hair.

"Oh thanks Ro Ro. Don't know how long I'll be able to teeter around on these heels, though! Anyway, I think we all look pretty amazing!"

Claire had opted for a loose-fit backless deep red dress which highlighted her blonde locks. Rosa and Dawn both wore slinky trousers with strappy tops. They were be-jewelled and ready to party!

They started in one of the bars, had some lethal cocktails then went on to a nightclub. Lucy and Dawn were throwing themselves about on the dance floor when Lucy felt a tug on her arm and looked straight into Luigi's eyes as he pulled her round to face him. Her heart gave a huge lurch, suddenly they were dancing.

Dawn smiled and carried on dancing around with whoever was willing to dance with her.

As Luigi pulled her towards him, Lucy just melted into his arms. It didn't matter that everyone else was busting some wild moves, they just swayed together, holding onto each other, totally oblivious of everyone else. Then he tentatively kissed her, gently, softly. Her stomach did cartwheels!

Rosa and Claire, who were all danced out, sitting quietly drinking themselves into a happy stupor, saw all this, nudged each other and slurred, "Told her sho, din we? Knew they'd get it on!"

Rosa, who had drunk a pint of water before going to bed, her magic formula for preventing a hangover, found the next morning that it hadn't worked all that well! Claire had spent an awful lot of the night hugging the toilet, Dawn collapsed into bed and died, snoring so loudly that if the others hadn't have been in the state they were in, they'd have not slept at all and Lucy… well, Lucy had spent the night having the most lurid and sensual dreams and now seemed to be floating around in a perpetual daze!

Somehow they managed to get themselves out of the hotel and onto the coach, looking decidedly jaded as it made its way to the airport. They even had a job to muster up their usual enthusiasm for browsing in the duty-free shops! But they each bought themselves some perfume, Dawn bought her mum's favourite for her as well. Although the flight wasn't all that long, all of them slept for the time it did take and were feeling a lot more human by the time they landed.

Lucy dropped them off one by one – well, two by one, as Dawn and Rosa shared an apartment together. She dropped Claire off last. "Certainly been an eventful holiday, hasn't it? I can't imagine what a turmoil your mind must be in right now. Are you going to be okay?"

"I'll be fine, Luce, don't worry, but yes, it was certainly a different holiday that's for sure, but it was so good to be all together even so, wasn't it?"

9

Darren was just leaving the chief accountant's office when he came along the corridor. "Looking for me, Darren?" he asked.

"No, it's okay, Will. I thought I'd left a file on your desk but it's not there. I'll have another look in my tray. I've probably buried it, knowing me!" Darren said with a cheery grin.

"What file was that, then?"

He had to think quickly. "Oh, some figures you asked me for last week but I hadn't finalised them all, do you remember?"

"Vaguely," Will replied.

"Anyway, I'll find it and bring it to you when I do, okay?"

Will walked into his office looking slightly puzzled and Darren wasn't entirely sure whether he had got away with it or not. Will was one of the three other British guys working in this section of the company and Darren always thought that, considering he was the chief accountant of that section, he wasn't the brightest spark and was sometimes away with the fairies. Darren suspected he tried the 'merchandise' occasionally so had gambled on his vagueness by inventing a file!

'Shit! I thought he was out to lunch!' he thought, as he went back to his desk. He took the USB stick from his wallet and put it in the hidden compartment in his briefcase. His mobile rang, 'number unknown' came up, Gio with a throwaway he thought. "Hello?"

"Meet me in the usual place tonight, handsome."

"Sorry, I think you have the wrong number mate!"

When he got back to his room, Darren opened his laptop and inserted the memory stick. As he scrolled down, he came upon some sets of figures. "Gotcha you bastard!" he said, triumphantly. He took out the USB, put it in a little envelope inside a birthday card, addressed it to Miss D. Brown, at an address in Dartford, Kent, England and dropped into the local courier with it. "Can you make sure that goes asap mate, it's my niece's birthday and I totally forgot! My niece will forgive me but my sister won't!"

The guy laughed. "You 'ave a sister like me 'ave! No worry, I send fast."

Darren patted him on the shoulder. "Lifesaver! Grazie," he said and strolled out.

When he met up with Gio later, they both had a lot to report. Gio had found out who the friend of the dead girl was and where she lived. He'd kept up a surveillance of her until she went to a bar local to her and followed her in. He 'accidently' bumped into her, causing her to spill her drink and made a big show of apologising, insisting that he buy her another and struck up a conversation with her. She was English.

"Had a bad day?" he'd asked. "You look a bit down in the dumps."

"Oh, no not really, it's just been a bit of a sad time lately."

"Oh, sorry to hear that." He waited for her to expand on this, hoping she would.

"I lost my best friend recently," she eventually said.

"Oh that sucks! I'm sorry, had she been ill?"

"No, she drowned."

"Oh Christ! That's bloody awful! That must have been a shock."

"It was, because she was a brilliant swimmer and it seems a mystery as to how she could have drowned. The polizia are still making enquiries. Sorry, I don't know why I'm telling you all this! I should have said I'm actually meeting someone."

"Oh it really was accidental when I bumped into you, not a pick-up ploy! I'm happily engaged, but sometimes it's good to get things off your chest and who better than a total stranger to tell it all to?" He smiled at her, willing her to continue.

"She had done so well in her job and had recently had a promotion."

"What did she do?" Gio prompted.

"She worked for the big pharmaceutical company over the bridge, in the distribution centre. She was very good at her job, very conscientious and efficient, I wasn't surprised she'd been promoted."

"Oh, yes I know it, probably a good place to work, drugs and medication are a big business."

"I guess so. We were due to meet up on the night that she died." A tear escaped down her cheek. "She said she needed to tell me something she was worried about."

"Oh, I'm sorry, it's very upsetting for you to talk about this. She didn't tell you what, then? That is sad. Look, I'm really sorry but I have to go now. I hope it's helped for you to talk it out."

"It has actually, thank you for listening."

"You're very welcome. Take care, ciao."

~

Gio recounted all of this to Darren. "The girl obviously stumbled on something she shouldn't have and was killed to keep it quiet," he said.

Gio agreed. "So how did you get on with tracking down the money?"

10

As soon as they were back from their holiday, Lucy enrolled herself into evening classes to learn Italian, much to the amusement of her friends.

Claire threw herself back into her work. It was a challenging job working in a school for children with special needs but there was nothing like seeing those children having such courage and determination and mostly with great humour to bring her down to earth and not dwell on her own problems. Of course, it was different when she went home and had just her own thoughts and memories. She relived over and over the time she had spent with Darren in Italy and time and time again tried to tell herself to accept the fact that she might not see him again but, try as she might, she could not. She knew he had said to get on with her life, to meet someone else, but she just couldn't!

When Claire and Lucy met up for coffee one Saturday, Lucy was worried by Claire's pale and drawn appearance. "Are you okay?" she demanded, after they'd hugged tightly.

"I'm okay," Claire replied.

"Well, sorry but you don't look it, lovey. Why don't you think again about coming to stay with me? I do get why you said no when I offered before, that you had to get on with your life, but really I do wish you would—"

Lucy was stopped by Claire's hand on her arm. "Luce, Luce, it's not that, it's not that!"

"Well what is it then? Has something happened? You're not ill are you?"

"I'm pregnant!" Claire whispered.

"Pregnant? Are you sure?"

Claire's lip quivered. "Yes, I've done the test twice, been puking like a good 'un every morning, my boobs are tender and yes, yes I'm quite sure!"

11

After months of detective work, Darren and Gio had uncovered the whole gang of people involved in the money-laundering swindle. It took some time to finalise it all as there were so many implicated, from those in the pharmaceutical company distributing the cocaine, to the different accountants as the money went through the different banks of the companies involved. Each link of the chain getting what they thought was a generous portion of the money but really none of those lower in the chain had a clue of the amount of money those at the top were getting.

The poor young girl had got caught up in it when she found a discrepancy and queried it with the head of the company. He told her he was very grateful to her for bringing it to his attention and after making sure that she hadn't yet told anyone else asked her to not mention it to anyone at all as he would need to have it investigated and wouldn't want to warn the guilty party.

"You've done extremely well to spot that, well done!" he said, as he guided her from his office. As soon as she was out of earshot he took a mobile phone from a locked drawer and dialled a number. "We have a big problem, I want you to sort it!" he said into the phone. "I'll send you the details." He slammed the phone back into the drawer and locked it, then paced the floor. Running his hands through his hair, he thumped his desk. "Fuck it!!" he bellowed.

When it was all over, Darren was released from his undercover persona but not until he had said his goodbyes to Gio. "It's been great working with you, Gio. We won't see each other again."

"You too, Darren. Be happy!"

Back in the UK, David was glad to be able to get back to being David Eastman, back to living in his own place, back to being away from central London. After he had been de-briefed, and was officially off the case, he had his hair cut back to his style, and the highlights that he liked put back in, removed the painful contact lenses (he'd never found them comfortable), put his favourite designer specs on and shaved off the stubble. It occurred to him that even if Claire had not found anyone else she may not like the look of David, having fallen in love with Darren!

The next thing David did was to visit his parents.

"Oh mum, don't cry. I'm here now!" He hugged them both.

His dad said, in a voice gruff with emotion, "Glad you're back safe and sound, son. I know we can't ask anything about where you've been, or what you had to do, but did it all go as it should?"

"Yes dad, couldn't have gone better actually. Now, how are you both? What have you been up to? Tell me all your news."

∿

Rosa came home in a state of excitement. "Dawnie! Dawnie! Are you home?"

"Yes, I'm in the loo. What's the panic?"

"Hurry up and finish, then. I've got something to tell you – well, two things to tell you, actually!"

Dawn came out of the toilet, drying her hands as she went. "Cor, you're wound up. What's going on?"

"Well, there's good news and bad news. I'll tell you the bad first and get that out of the way. You know the guy, Toby, in the office who has the mate with a sister in Italy?"

"Yes, he's the one that found out about the holiday for us, isn't he?"

"Well, I haven't seen him for ages as he was seconded to another area and when he came back today, he was asking me if we had a good time and all that, THEN said that his mate's sister had been murdered! She was the girl on the beach!"

"Oh my God that's awful!" Dawn said. "Do they know who did it and why?"

"Well, he said it was not reported much and it's not clear why, but there is a big investigation going on and it's something to do with the pharmaceutical company she worked for!"

"Blimey, we didn't realise we were in amongst that, did we?" They both pondered for a while, then Dawn asked, "So what's the good news? You said there was good news!"

"Oh there is. I bumped into Lucy coming out of the market. She said she was going to pop round later with some news, but I couldn't wait so persuaded her to tell me then."

"Well, don't keep me in suspense! What was it?!"

"Claire's pregnant! She said it was okay for Lucy to tell us."

"Claire's pregnant?! How? I mean I know how, but who with?"

12

David saw a strange car in the drive of his parents' house as he pulled up. When he let himself in and before he called out, "Hi Mum it's me!" as he always did, he thought he recognised a woman's voice, one that he hadn't heard for a good number of years, about five he reckoned.

He found them all in the kitchen diner. "Oh here he is!" his mum sang out, rather weirdly, David thought. "Look who's come to see us!"

David looked guardedly at Anna. Their break-up all those years before hadn't been at all pleasant. He'd broken up with her after a six-month relationship, and she'd not taken it very well but both had gone their separate ways and he'd heard she'd married some guy from London.

"Hello Anna, long time no see," he said coolly. She had taken on a more sophisticated style and looked very well dressed, he noted. Her clothes looked expensive.

"Hello David, how are you?"

It was all very stilted. "We're just having coffee darling, I'll make you a cup," his mum said, in an effort to lighten the atmosphere.

"Good day at the office son?" his dad asked, as always in such a way without asking David what he'd actually been doing.

"Not bad dad, got to get back into the swing after the long break I've had."

Anna broke in awkwardly. "David, I wonder if we could go somewhere for a coffee or something as there's something I'd like to discuss with you, that I'd like your help with if possible. Sorry Barbara," she said to David's mum. "I don't mean to be rude but it's quite a private matter."

Despite the internal tussle, David was sitting at a table across from Anna at a coffee shop in the square. David had ordered himself a black coffee. "So what did you want to talk about?"

"My husband is in prison."

"Oh God, I'm sorry to hear that!"

"Well it's his own stupid, greedy fault and in fact I'm filing for divorce, but that's another story. The thing is, I think there's someone watching the house. He wasn't happy when I sent the divorce papers to him and I don't know if it's anything to do with that. I know you can't officially do anything, David, but to be honest I'm a bit scared."

"Have you notified the police?"

"They'd think I'm just being neurotic but I've seen a car parked across the road from my house and also seen it in the office car park."

"Did it follow you here?"

"I don't think so, I didn't see it."

"Why do you think it's anything to do with your husband?"

"That's one of the things I wanted to ask you about. Why do you think he'd have someone watching me?"

"I have no idea, Anna. I don't know what trouble he'd got into to end up in prison and to be honest I don't know what you think I can do to help!"

Anna had always been a panicker and sometimes a bit clingy, which was one of the reasons David had realised the relationship wasn't working for him. With Claire, it was very different. She was a gentle soul, so loving and giving and she never thought it was all about her.

Seeing Anna's crestfallen face, he said, "I really don't know what I can do to help and to be frank I'm not sure why you've contacted me, but I'll see if I can find anything out. You realise I can't jeopardise my job in any way?"

"Oh thank you!" she gushed. "Yes of course, I wouldn't want you to get into trouble."

"Can you jot down his name and what prison he's in?"

Anna got a notepad and pen out of her bag, wrote down the details, tore the page out and handed it to David. When David glanced at the name *Jason Montgomery*, he coolly returned his gaze to Anna and put the paper in his pocket.

"So what was his line of work then?" David casually asked.

"He's an accountant. I got him a job with the cosmetics company I work for. I'm their main buyer now," she said proudly. "He was made redundant from the company he was working for when we first got married."

David's mind worked furiously. "Oh right, okay Anna, as I said I really don't know what I can do, but leave it with me and don't expect much, I'm not promising anything. You'd better give me a contact number in case I do have anything to report."

"Yes of course and thank you for taking the time to listen."

She handed him a business card, lightly touching his arm as she did so.

David quickly withdrew his arm, took the card, said his goodbyes and left.

13

If Claire had to be a single mum, so be it. She couldn't keep pining on about Darren. She had to think of the baby now, so she had made up her mind to just concentrate on that and put Darren to the back of her mind.

Her parents were being very supportive. She hadn't gone into details, they didn't know about her meeting with Darren, only that it was a holiday romance. She would tell them all if her and Darren were ever able to be together, but for now it was all they needed to know. They were brilliant parents, hadn't gone ballistic at her, just made sure having the baby was what she wanted and her mum had just said, "Oh well, these things happen and you know dad and I are here for you." They had even given her enough money to put down the first six months' rent on a bigger apartment and her dad had helped her to decorate the little box-room as a nursery.

Because her new job meant she could work from home as long as she went into the office once a week for meetings, she could fit it in around the baby, although her mum had already said she would help out for babysitting duties if needed, so all in all Claire was in a good place for the first time in a long while.

In fact, she had agreed to go out for the evening with Lucy, Rosa and Dawn.

David had arranged to meet his mate Ben, who was in the Met, in a bar on the other side of the Thames as he didn't want to take any chances in coming up against anyone that he'd met when undercover.

While he was waiting for Ben, he heard some giggling as four girls came into the bar. He spluttered into his drink when he recognised Claire and her friends. His heart did a lurch and he was working out how to approach her, knowing that she wouldn't recognise him, when one of the girls moved to one side to put her bag on the table and he was shocked to see that Claire was unmistakably pregnant!

So, she had taken him at his word and found someone else. His mind was racing. She must have found someone straight away to be so evidently pregnant. He had a hard knot in his stomach. 'What else did you expect?' he asked himself.

Ben jolted him out of his thoughts, banging his greeting on his shoulder.

"Christ Ben, you frightened the life out of me!"

Claire jerked her head round. "You okay?" Lucy asked. "You've gone a bit pale, have you got a pain or something? Claire!"

"Oh ermm no Luce, no, I haven't got a pain. It was just

when that guy at the bar spoke to his mate just then it made my stomach lurch as it sounded just like Darren!"

"Which one?"

"The one in the specs with the blonde highlights."

Lucy followed Claire's gaze. "Well, it certainly isn't Darren but *very* nice!"

"Oh, stop Luce! It just gave me a funny turn. He even has mannerisms like Darren."

"You've obviously not pushed Darren as far back in your mind as you thought you had, honey! Come on, let's find a seat."

~

"So what's this all about then, Dave? Dave! Hello! Earth to Dave!"

"Oh, sorry mate, I had a bit of a shock just now. Let's go round the other side in the corner." David knew he'd be unable to concentrate if he still had Claire in his eye-line, and he and Ben had a lot to discuss.

"So this ex-girlfriend of yours is the wife of Jason Montgomery?" Ben asked, after they'd settled in a new spot.

"Yes, I had no idea who she'd married, didn't have any more to do with her once we'd split up. She knew a whole different crowd to me so our paths never crossed."

"So what's the problem then?"

David explained what Anna had told him. "Don't get me wrong, Ben. I don't want to get involved with her, or her problems with her husband, but I'm curious as to why he's got someone watching her. Weren't any loose ends left when that job was wound up?"

"What, are you thinking she had some input in there somewhere? You think he's got unfinished business there?"

"I don't know, mate. Just wondered if you'd think it was worth a look, worth taking to your chief or not?"

"Leave it with me, I'll make a few enquiries and will keep you up to speed. I've gotta shoot off now Dave, but I'll get on it and be in touch."

"Thanks Ben, see ya."

When Claire looked up again, the guy was no longer at the bar, but the incident had left her feeling unsettled. She needed to calm herself down a bit.

"Be back in a minute girls, yet another trip to the loo!" she laughed. As she rounded the corner heading for the ladies, she bumped straight into the guy from the bar as he was walking away from his table. She couldn't help but put a protective hand over her bump.

"Oh, I'm sorry!" he said. "Are you okay, Clairey?"

Fuck, he thought, why did I say that! Nobody else ever called Claire that except him.

"D... Darren?" she said hesitantly, stumbling back a little.

He caught hold of her arm. "Steady! Actually, it's not Darren, it's David, but yes, it's me. Are you okay? Can we talk?"

"Of course, but hang on a minute can you? I'll just go tell the girls to carry on without me."

Claire went back to the girls, quickly explained that she had bumped into Darren and told them to enjoy their evening.

"I was right about the guy at the bar, it was him!"

Claire assured her friends she'd be okay and that she would let them know what happened when they spoke later, and went back to David.

"Wow!" Rosa exclaimed. "That's a turn-up. Must admit, I didn't think she'd see him again."

"I do hope she isn't going to be hurt again!" Lucy said worriedly.

Dawn put her arm through Lucy's. "I think Claire's a lot stronger than we give her credit for. Now, are we going to get another drink or what?"

"Before anything else, I want to say that I am now free from the job I was doing and was going to give you a ring while I'm in London to see if you wanted to meet, or to see if you'd found someone else and I see that you have," David said, nodding to her bump. "And I'm pleased you didn't just waste your life waiting around, although I wouldn't be honest if I didn't say that I'd hoped you would!"

Before he could continue, Claire grabbed his hand. "Darren, I mean David, stop! I haven't met anyone else, didn't want to."

"But…"

"Shush a minute!" She tightened her grip on his hand. "This…" she said, encircling her little bump with her other hand and then patting it gently, "Is *our* baby. *You* are the father!"

She saw so many emotions working their way round his face. It was strange that, although Dar, erm David, she corrected her thoughts, looked outwardly so different, she felt instantly the same feelings and kind of liked this different version. Although she missed seeing his eyes without the glasses, they did suit him, as did his hair!

She waited for him to arrange his feelings and emotions and to speak when he was ready to do so. She had rehearsed many times how to handle this situation, if it was to happen, and had determined to not say anything until David spoke, not wanting to interrupt, or influence, his thoughts, and eventually he did speak.

"So, in Italy, when we ermm…"

"… And I'm going to be a dad?"

"And were you going to tell me?"

"I was waiting to see if you were in a position to contact me Darr, I mean David. When I was escorted back to my hotel your last words to me were that you didn't know when or if we would be able to be together again!" Claire said hotly.

"I know and I'm sorry I had to leave it like that but I was honestly thinking of your safety… wow!" He looked completely dazed.

"Is that a good wow, or an 'I don't believe it' wow?"

There was a pause. Claire was feeling even more unsettled. Did this mean the end of them? She had got used to the idea that she was going to be a single parent but oh, she had so secretly hoped that they could be parents together. Suddenly David pulled her to him, kissed her passionately and said, "It's a wow kind of wow! God I've missed you, Claire… and we're going to have a baby!" He laughed as he pulled her away to look at her.

14

B en's superior said he could go through the files of the case as long as he did it in his own time.

"You know we're short of men at the moment so I can't afford for you taking time up that would be spent on other duties on a case that's over and done with; if you think there's more to come you can take some of your own time to go through it, but don't let your other work suffer, we've plenty of current cases to work on!"

So when he was off-duty, he started on the first files and rang David. "Can you come to the station? I've gotta look at the files in my own time and it'll be quicker with us both going through them."

"Ermm, what right now?"

"You got something better to do then, lucky sod?"

"Well I have, but it's okay I'll be there in half an hour."

Ben and David waded through the files for three hours. "Well there's nothing that indicates we missed anything that I can see, what about you?"

It all seemed done and dusted.

"Did we check every phone record? I mean, because we had them all bang to rights and the case was solved and they were all convicted, could we have got a bit lax with some of the minor details d'ya reckon?"

As he checked yet another sheet which was all cleared, David slapped down the papers he was looking at. "Forget it. Probably got nothing to do with the case at all."

"Wait Dave, what's this?" Ben showed David the paper he'd been studying. "Someone has noted at the side of this 'cosmetics warehouse'."

"That's interesting. What's the address?" Ben showed him. "That's the cosmetics company Jason put some of the money through and where Anna works. Said she's head buyer. We must have done a full research, mustn't we?"

"Buggered if I know. You think there's more going on there and that's why he's having her followed?"

"Your guess is as good as mine, but we must have cleared it all at the time. We were pretty sure he wasn't involved at the meaty end."

Lucy was making slow but steady progress with her Italian lessons. She'd also built up a lot of flexihours to use up, so she made what was for her a pretty hasty decision to book another trip. If she went on a Friday and returned on the Tuesday, it would give her a nice long weekend. She had enough leave to cover the three days that were either side of the weekend and had found some good deals online. She was a bit nervous about the fact that she would have to go on her own as Claire wouldn't be wanting to fly in her pregnant state and in any case she was at the start of her relationship with David and needed to concentrate on that. Neither Dawn nor Rosa had any more leave to take until later in the year. She had to be brave and go on her own.

She decided not to tell Luigi she was coming. She wanted to see his reaction and be sure that he was genuine about wanting to see her again. It was a risky decision but she would know then if she was just a dalliance to him. What she really dreaded was getting there and finding him ensconced in a romance with another holidaymaker.

She'd never flown on her own before so the whole thing was pretty nerve-wracking but also made her tingle with excitement and anticipation.

Ben's superior listened with muted interest. "I don't know if I want you using your time up looking into this, Ben. You know we've got those three big cases going on at the moment and if there were any mileage in it, I reckon it would have been followed up at the time, wouldn't it?"

"I know, guv. I realise we're stacked out. I'll tell Dave to let it go."

After some thought, his chief said, "Look, I don't like the thought something might have been missed. You've got to go and check out that lead on the jewellery heist, which isn't too far from where that warehouse is, is it? So you can take an hour out to just check it over, okay? Just don't ruffle any feathers!"

Ben parked in the car park next to the warehouse, removed his jacket, rolled up his shirt sleeves and messed his hair up a bit. He meandered into the warehouse, looking vaguely around him.

"Can I help you, mate?" asked a young chap in grey overalls carrying a clipboard.

"Oh hiya, I was given this address as a storage space but I think there's been some mistake, this doesn't look like a storage shed," Ben replied with a grin.

The young man grinned back. "Well, not unless you want to store your nail varnish. It's a cosmetics warehouse!"

"Bloody hell, is it? Definitely can't store my gear in here, then. No nail varnish in it, that's for sure! You don't think about cosmetics needing a warehouse, do you? Mind you, the amount my missus spends on the stuff, she could fill one on her own I reckon!" They both laughed.

Ben had been looking around all the time they'd been talking and had seen the guy in a suit watching them from the window of an office that overlooked the warehouse floor. "Well, thanks a lot for your time, mate. I'll let you get on and I'll get back and check the address. Cheers!"

"Sure you're okay about the baby?" She'd sensed he was a bit edgy and wondered if he'd had time to think about it and had second thoughts. It had been a lot for him to take on board.

"Of course I am, but we need to chat about it all. What arrangements we need to make, where we'll live and, oh yes, the other thing is…" He slid off the sofa onto the floor, turned towards her, held her hand and said, "Will you marry me?"

Claire caught her breath. "You don't have to do that. I don't mind being an unmarried mother!"

"I'm not asking because you're pregnant, I'm asking because I love you and want us to be husband and wife. Don't you want that too?"

He waited what seemed like hours but in fact was just a few seconds before Claire threw her arms around his neck and said, "YES!"

He produced a ring from his pocket and as he put it on her finger said, "Don't do that to me! You had me worried!"

Claire laughed her throaty laugh, which, of course, he always found such a turn-on.

"You don't know how nervous I was!"

She pulled him back up onto the sofa and kissed him, looking down at her finger and the gorgeous ring glistening on it. "It's beautiful! I love it!" Then gave him another passionate kiss. "I can't wait to be your wife!" she said, her eyes shining with emotion.

As David held her, she recognised that fire in his eyes. "Is it safe? I mean for the baby?" he asked.

She removed his shirt and undid his jeans, whispering in his ear, "Most definitely!"

Later, after they'd showered and were in soft towelling robes, they decided to look at some wedding pages on the internet. When they were scrolling through, Claire said, "How did you know the ring would fit?"

"Ah, well, a bit of subterfuge, aided by your mum. By the way, I did ask for their blessing to ask you and they gave it."

Claire was surprised as her mum had not let on a thing when she saw her that morning and she was not known for being able to keep secrets.

15

D avid met with Anna to update her. He hadn't mentioned his meeting to Claire, he wasn't exactly sure why, but he didn't like to involve her in his work and this was about work, he told himself. He also hoped he could get it sorted without Claire ever needing to know Anna was an ex-girlfriend.

"So have you found out why he's having me watched?" Anna asked.

"Not yet, no, but who do you deal with when you're buying your cosmetics?"

"What do you mean?"

"Well, is it a certain company? A certain country? Or do they come from all over the world?"

"Wherever I get a good price to ensure we get a good turnover. Why? What's this got to do with anything?"

"It might not have anything to do with anything, but you asked me to look into things and that's what I'm doing."

Anna put her hand over his. "I do appreciate you doing this for me."

Claire had decided at the last minute to go and check out a wedding dress shop that Dawn had told her about. Someone Dawn worked with had recommended it as they specialised in 'different' needs, such as a dress for a pregnant bride, not such an unusual occurrence as it used to be. She was a bit bogged down with a project she was working on, needed to clear her head to have a re-think, so had given herself some time off work to go and check it out, thinking if it looked a possibility, her and her mum could have a day out there together. She took the train to London and she found the street where the shop was supposed to be. She was scanning the shops over the road, trying to find the wedding shop when her heart gave a pleasurable lurch as she saw David sitting at a table in a coffee shop, but then saw he was sitting with an attractive dark-haired woman. 'Don't be silly Claire, he meets all kinds of people in his job,' she told herself irritably.

She tried to regulate her breathing as her thoughts meandered on and then she looked away quickly, with tears pricking her eyes, as the woman tenderly put her hand over David's.

She didn't stay to see David jerk his hand away.

16

From the moment he first saw her, Jason Montgomery was besotted with Anna. He couldn't believe it and was over the moon when she agreed to marry him. He already knew that she was needy and rather spoilt with expensive tastes, but he didn't care. He gave her everything she wanted. Fine clothes, nice home, jewellery, took her to fine restaurants and they were happy together, but he needed to earn well to do so and after he was made redundant, although all was well to start with while he had his redundancy money, when it started to dwindle because he continued to pander to her whims, he could see her becoming less than happy. It helped, of course, when he got the accountancy job with the cosmetics company that she worked for, and he thought all would be okay again and for a little while it was.

It soon became apparent, however, that what he was earning in the job was not enough for the lifestyle she had become used to and expected. He knew it was partly his fault for always indulging her but also knew he would soon lose her if he didn't come up with more money to feed her needs, so when he was approached and given the option of a £100,000 lump sum for just fudging a few figures, although he knew, of course, that it had to be something illegal, he gave in to the temptation in order to keep her. He might have known that to receive that kind of money what he had been asked to do was probably highly risky, but he thought she was worth the risk. He had no idea why he had to fudge the figures and didn't ask any questions. He just saw it as a way of keeping Anna.

'A lot of good it did, I've lost her anyway,' he told himself afterwards. Jason was no big crook and was very small-fry in the organisation, hence his small, in comparison to the millions changing hands, payout. He wouldn't be in prison as long as some of the others, the 'big boys', but he had to pay for the part he had played. Oh, he didn't really blame her for wanting the divorce, he knew it wasn't in her character to be the kind of wife that would wait for him. It saddened him that his efforts to keep her had probably lost him any chance of doing so, but he did still love her and worried that she might be dragged into it somehow. One of his mates said he knew someone that wouldn't mind earning a few bob watching the house a bit. Little did Jason know that this attempt to keep Anna out of it was to do the exact opposite!

Lucy couldn't believe that she was being bold enough to just fly off to Italy on her own and wasn't at all sure how her long weekend would unfold.

She'd had a text from Claire while she was in the departure lounge, wishing her a safe trip and hoping all would work out how she wanted.

Thanks honey, you and D have fun wedding planning wknd!! Lucy replied.

Claire's reply was not as enthusiastic as Lucy expected.

Anything wrong? she sent back.

Just me being silly, saw D in coffee bar with woman.

Oh hun it was prob to do with work!!

Claire agreed and told her to have fun in Italy.

"Clairey? Did you hear what I said?"

"Oh, I'm sorry, I was miles away, what did you say?"

"I said mum and dad have invited us over for supper tomorrow, is that okay with you?"

"Oh, yes of course, that'll be lovely!"

"Are you sure you're okay?"

"I told you I'm fine, stop worrying!"

David wasn't convinced. She had been unusually distracted lately. He hoped there wasn't anything wrong with the baby that she wasn't telling him.

They were in the middle of the supper at David's parents' when the doorbell rang. "Who could that be?" his mum said as she put her wine glass down. "No darling I'll go," she said as David's dad got up to answer the door.

"Oh! Anna!" she said in surprise. "Hello, is something wrong?" Barbara Eastman was a mild mannered, softly spoken woman but was a staunch protector of her family. She had never much cared for Anna when David had dated her and didn't want her spoiling their evening.

There was a guffaw of laughter from the dining room. "Oh I'm sorry, have you got guests?" Anna asked.

"Yes, David and his fiancée are eating with us and actually

we're right in the middle of our meal, Anna. What can I do for you?"

"Fiancée? I didn't realise David was engaged!"

"Yes, to a lovely girl too."

"Actually, I wondered if he was here as I wanted to have a quick word with him if that's okay?"

"Well, if it isn't too urgent, could it wait, Anna? As I said, we're in the middle of our meal."

David came to see where his mum had got to. "Your food's getting cold, mum… oh! Anna."

Barbara turned towards her son, raised her eyes heavenwards and said, "Anna wanted a word with you but I've explained that we're in the middle of our meal," she said pointedly.

David had left the door ajar and Claire could see who they were speaking to. She recognised the woman from the coffee shop and her knife clattered to the floor. "Ssorry!" she said as they all jumped. She scrambled, red faced, to the floor to pick it up.

"I'd better come back another time, I'm sorry I've interrupted your evening," Anna said. She could see the annoyance on David's face and she turned to go.

"You could have rung me, Anna, you have my number!" David said sharply.

"Yes, yes I'll do that, bye," she said over her shoulder and hurried down the drive to her car with tears pricking her eyes. She sat in her car and hammered the steering wheel with her hands as tears of anger flowed. That hadn't gone at all as she had planned!

Later, when they were on their own, Claire broached the subject. "Who was that at your parents' door?" She took a deep breath; knew it wasn't good for the baby to withhold her worries. "I saw you the other day in the coffee shop with her."

David took hold of her hands. "Oh! Is *that* why you've been quiet? You daft thing. You have nothing to worry about in that quarter, I can tell you! You have nothing to worry about full stop, you know how much I love you... both," he said, patting her tummy. He then explained about Anna, without going into too many details of the police side of things.

"I'm sorry I doubted you, it's the baby hormones," she said as she threw her arms around his neck.

Once again, David wished he had never got involved in Anna's problems.

'Whatever possessed me to do this?' Lucy asked herself, realising she had made this hasty decision like a lovesick teenager.

Once she had settled into her hotel room she decided, as it was the middle of the afternoon, to have a wander into town. It felt strange being back here without the others but at least she knew her way around. Without aiming to, she found herself across the road from the polizia.

'Now what do I do?' she wondered. She didn't even know if Luigi was on duty today. 'This is ridiculous!' she told herself, and turned to retrace her steps and ambled in the direction of the beach. She wandered for a while, then made her way back to the hotel, determined to start acting in a more mature manner!

She ate dinner in the hotel restaurant, then decided to relax in her room for the evening – well, as far as she could relax!

She tried to read a magazine she'd bought at the airport but couldn't concentrate. Finally she thought, 'Sod it, I didn't come here to sit in a hotel room!' She showered, sorted out a suitable outfit and made her way outside. However, once in the town her courage left her. She wasn't used to going in bars on her own at home, let alone in any other country. As she was trying to make her mind up whether or not to go into the bar that she knew Luigi visited or to turn tail and go back, she saw him walking towards her with a group of others. She froze on the spot for a few seconds, then he saw her. "Luci!" He hurried towards her with a huge grin on his face. She suddenly felt very shy! "You come back!" He laughed, kissing her on the cheek.

"Vengo a trovarti."

"You learn Italiano!"

Lucy hoped that she had said, 'I come to see you'! He put his arm across her back to help her gently into the bar.

As Lucy felt the warmth of his hand as it clung to her waist and the tingle it shot through her, she had a feeling she had made the right decision after all.

17

Anna was quite hysterical on the phone. "I never asked you to have anything to do with where I work. My boss has had me in the office asking me if Jason has told me things! It was bad enough when the police kept questioning me when Jason got himself involved in all that trouble, how could he do that to me?!"

"For God's sake calm down, Anna. I haven't been anywhere near your work!"

"It's all very well for you to say calm down, I thought I'd done with all this. Bloody Jason, he's ruined my life."

"Obviously your little visit made someone worry or why would the gaffer have hauled Anna into his office?" David had met up with Ben to tell him about Anna's outburst.

"You think she knows anything?"

"The Anna I knew years ago certainly wouldn't have done and I don't think she does now or why would she have got me

70

involved?"

"True. We need to have a look in that warehouse but there's no way we'd get a search warrant. Think she could get you in there somehow?"

"I don't know about that, Ben. She might be a pain in the backside but I don't know if I want to get her involved in anything that might put her in danger all the same."

David was sitting in his car when Anna arrived. He waited and, sure enough, spotted a guy who was obviously following her. He saw the guy go in, see Anna and go over to a publicity stand and feign browsing the leaflets.

David moved his car to block the one the guy had arrived in, got his mobile out and sent Anna a text.

Sorry, change of plan. Can we meet in the lay-by opposite my parents' place?

He saw Anna come out and get in her car. Watching as the stranger followed her, David put his phone to his ear and loudly took part in an animated conversation. The guy rapped on his window.

"You've blocked me in! I need to get out!"

David put his hand up in apology and gestured five minutes with it.

"Move! I need to get out now!"

David slowly ended his call and wound down his window a fraction. "Sorry mate, I had to take that call. You know what it's like." Meanwhile he'd seen Anna leave the car park and turn into the road leading to his parents' place.

He judged enough time for her to be out of sight while the guy was fuming, "Fucking well move, will you!"

Eventually David, apologising again, did so.

"So why couldn't we meet in the motel?" Anna whined when David pulled in.

"Oh I remembered afterwards that one of Claire's friends sometimes works in reception, sorry about that. Wouldn't want her to think there's something going on between us."

The implication was clearly compelling. "What did you want to speak to me about, if it's not about Jason?" she asked tentatively.

"I want to do something special for Claire and it occurred to me that you might be able to help me with that because of your connection with cosmetics and stuff. Sort of a return of favour."

He had to play to her vanity again. "I'm sure being the head buyer you'd be able to help me pick something special, wouldn't you?"

18

Naturally, the warehouse was in darkness when they got there.

Anna let them in through a side door and switched off the alarm. "So what in particular do you want to look at?"

"Well, what's the most unusual item you have, anything in special packaging?" He cast his eyes about for anything out of the ordinary, noticed an advertising placard and a scuff mark on the floor. He sauntered over, pretending to glance about as he did.

Anna gave a loud sigh.

"Sorry, I'm being a pain, aren't I?" David said, fingering the placard. "What's this, a new line or something?" he asked, as he swung the placard about.

"Oops, sorry!" he said, as it fell to the floor. He noticed a small finger hole in the bit of wall behind it and some hinges that were so well camouflaged he nearly missed them.

"Hello, what's this – a hidey hole?" he said, pulling at the hole.

"For Christ's sake, David, this is getting beyond a joke now. What are you doing?"

"There's a little room here and a door with a padlock on it in there. What's in there then, the crown jewels?"

"I don't know, I don't ever buy anything that warrants that much security."

"Might just be where I find what I'm looking for, then. Can you get the key?"

"Oh bloody hell, David, there's a fucking warehouse full of stuff here. Surely you can find something in this lot!" Anna was fast losing her patience. She'd had plans for tonight and this wasn't part of them.

"Where's your sense of adventure?" he said, standing close enough for her to smell his familiar aftershave. She gave an involuntary shiver.

"Cold?" he asked, putting his arm around her shoulder.

"Perhaps a little," she simpered, looking up at him.

"Well perhaps we'll get warm in there, huh?" he said, lifting an eyebrow.

"I'll see if there's a key in the office. Won't be long," she said, giving him a lingering look before hurrying off.

Anna remembered once when she was in the office, seeing the manager quickly close a little tray that slotted under the desk. She felt for it, opened it and there was a key!

When she was out of sight, David sent a quick text to Ben. *Did you lose him?*

"I found this. Looks like a padlock key, doesn't it?"

"It does indeed," David replied and Anna felt a warm glow.

David tried the key and after a wiggle it opened the padlock. He pulled open the door and realised, too late, that it was alarmed.

"Dave?"

"Who's that?" Anna gasped.

"In here, Ben!"

"What's going on, David?" Anna was plainly confused.

"It's alarmed, Ben. I'm taking Anna out of here."

David whisked a dazed Anna out to his car and had just disappeared round the bend as the manager arrived. Ben came out through a side door and had just apprehended the guy when two squad cars arrived. Ben's chief let out a long, low, whistle of amazement and admiration when Ben showed him inside the store.

"You set me up, didn't you David? I know I might not be the brightest spark in the box but even I can work that out!" She pouted. "You made me look a fool!"

"I'm sorry Anna, I'm afraid I did – set you up, that is, not make you look foolish, I had no intention of doing that, but it's thanks to you that we have finally found the last piece of a jigsaw we thought we'd completed. If you hadn't have asked me to find out who was watching you, we would never have found that stash and it would have carried on, so thank you Anna."

"So how far was Jason involved? Did he know about all that stuff?"

"He really did only fudge the figures. I say only, of course it was very wrong and it's why he ended up in prison, but he has no criminal instincts in him. I went to see Jason and spoke to him about having you watched, and yes, he did have someone watch out for you, but only because he loves you and was worried about you being on your own. He called the guy off after."

Anna's lips trembled. "Was he alright?"

"As alright as you can be in prison, I guess."

"But I felt someone following me."

"Someone else was following you, but that was from your place of work. Listen, Jason only agreed to speak to me if I promised to get a message to you. He said he doesn't blame you for wanting the divorce after his stupidity and what he got himself into, but it doesn't stop him loving you. You do know, don't you, Anna that he only got involved in all that because he truly thought that you needed him to have more money in order for you to be happy?"

"So it's my fault, is it?" she said hotly.

"In a way, I suppose it is."

19

David's blunt, but gentle, talk resulted in Anna doing an awful lot of soul searching. Eventually, after much thought and deliberation, she came to the decision to go and see Jason. She hadn't done so since he went to prison and during her soul searching made another admission to herself – she was afraid of seeing him in there. She didn't know how to deal with it.

When she saw Jason, she felt a whole mixture of emotions, from sadness as he looked so worried and drawn, to embarrassment at having to visit him here. (Her soul searching hadn't quite dissolved her snobbery!)

But what surprised her most of all was that she also felt a stirring in her heart. She realised that she did still feel something for him, she did actually miss him and not just what he could give her. She didn't know whether they could ever get back to a happy marriage but she did think that perhaps she might delay the divorce for a while. "But don't get too hopeful, I just need time to think about everything, we'll see what happens," she told him.

It was the most beautiful wedding. Claire looked absolutely stunning in her beige dress with gold filigree running through the bodice, fitted snugly on the top of her bump and flowing elegantly down to her ankles.

"You look beautiful!" David said as she arrived at his side, his eyes shining with love.

Because David had wanted to finish the case before the wedding, they had just three weeks from their wedding day to the day their son was due to be born. Claire had said she didn't mind waiting until after but David was adamant that he didn't want their son to be born out of wedlock, which Claire thought charmingly old fashioned!

As chief bridesmaid, Lucy carried out her duties to the letter and Dawn and Rosa made up the glamorous trio of attendants. Dawn had found a new man, Adam. She had met him online and they had clicked as soon as they'd met in person. Rosa had been out with a few guys but she had yet to find THE one.

"You need someone that likes his food!" Dawn said.

"You're right there, perhaps I should date a chef!"

"Nah, you'd never see him."

"I'd eat well, though!"

Lucy loved hearing the banter between them all. They had all been friends for such a long time – her and Claire the longest, of course.

Due to the short notice they'd had to prepare for the wedding, they all agreed that a small, relaxed, family wedding was just perfect so they had hired a marquee and had it erected in David's parents' garden. Someone Rosa knew did the catering. They had only invited a select few friends and close family. It was simple and warmly wonderful!

Lucy was watching the laughing group of people dancing, with Claire and David in the middle and Claire attempting to bob about as best she could. As she concentrated on watching Claire with a fond smile, she saw Claire clutch her stomach and a pool of water appear on the floor.

Baby George Eastman was anxious to make his appearance!

20

Lucy's thoughts were fluttering about in unison with the wings of the butterfly she was watching. She sighed a contented sigh. She was so thrilled when Claire had asked her to be one of baby George's godparents. He was such a gorgeous little boy. "Well why wouldn't he be with such good looking parents?" she muttered.

'Life's funny sometimes,' she thought. 'Who knew that a girls' holiday in Italy could change the course of so many lives?'

She felt a pang of sadness for the family of the young girl that had been killed, just for being in the wrong place at the wrong time and doing her job so thoroughly.

The butterfly flew off to look elsewhere and a different bee came to look in the lavender. Lucy had a slurp of her coffee and sighed again, annoyed that she had lowered her mood. She could hear him stirring inside. He would come and find her soon, and even the thought of it lifted her mood. She sighed a happier sigh. That trip certainly did change the course of her life!

She heard the door to the terrace open and waited for him

to find her and put his arms around her. As he did so, he bent and kissed her neck. She shivered with delight.

"Buongiorno mia bella moglie!" he whispered in her ear.

She turned and lifted her face to his, "Buongiorno, mio bel marito." His lips found hers.

Oh yes, her mood was definitely lifted.

Out of Sri Lanka

1

_____

Diana, standing at the window, looked down at her beautiful daughter, Louisa, as she was taking things out to her car. Diana felt a knot in her stomach. She was going to miss her so much while she was at university. Louisa looked up. She knew her mum would be standing there, knew she would be feeling sad. She waved. Diana opened the window and shouted, "I'm just coming, darling."

Louisa's skin was the colour of pale milk chocolate, her hair black and glossy, her almond-shaped eyes were dark, bright and alert. Diana had told her at a very early age that she was adopted and when Louisa had asked the inevitable question of why she didn't have an adopted dad, Diana had explained to her that she had split up with her partner before the adoption process was finalised. They had parted without malice, she'd told Louisa. He just wasn't ready to be a dad.

"But I was so very lucky because I was able to adopt you on my own!" Diana had said triumphantly and hugged Louisa tightly.

"Are you sure you've packed enough warm clothes, Lou?"

"Yess mum! I've packed plenty of warm clothes, I'm not going to the arctic!"

"I know, I know, I'm fussing, I can't help it," Diana said and felt her eyes becoming moist.

"Oh mum, I'll be back home for the holidays before you know it," Louisa said, hugging her mum tightly.

Diana sniffed, swallowed, cleared her throat, blinked hard, determined not to see her beloved daughter off in tears. "Right then, let's get the last of this stuff in the boot. Are you sure you haven't got a whole apartment there and not just a small room? You've got enough stuff to fill one!"

Louisa grinned. "It looks a lot but it really is just the essentials, mum."

Diana eyed the bag full of shoes, rolled her eyes and said, "I'm sure it is, darling!" They both laughed.

Eventually the car was all packed and the time had come. "You will text me when you arrive, won't you?"

"Of course I will, mum. You're going to be alright here on your own, aren't you?" Louisa felt a pang of guilt as she realised she had been so consumed with her excitement, mixed with a few nerves, that she hadn't really considered the fact that her mum might not be okay here on her own.

"Of course I will, silly, I've got lots of things planned to keep me busy when I'm not at work, don't you worry," Diana said with a confidence she didn't truly feel.

Diana kept it together as she waved Louisa out of the cul-de-sac, then dissolved into tears as she went in the house and closed the door. She went straight to Louisa's bedroom and sat on her bed. She was so very proud of her daughter and what she had achieved, but it was through no small sacrifice on

Diana's part. She had worked hard to give Louisa all that she could as she was growing up, never wanting her to suffer because she only had one parent.

Louisa often asked her, "Why don't you go out, mum? Go out for a drink with the girls. You never know, you might meet someone!"

Diana didn't really have 'girls' to go out with and usually made some excuse for not doing so. She did do so occasionally and did sometimes meet someone, but nothing ever came of it. Louisa was an intelligent girl and knew very well what sacrifices her mum had made for her.

"One day, mum, I'll be able to repay all that you've done for me."

"Oh don't talk like that, Lou," Diana had said, hugging her daughter and stroking her hair fondly. "You're my daughter, it's called looking after my child, it's what parents do and they don't need repaying!"

She'd been a pretty easy-going mum. Yes, they'd had the odd fallout, of course they had, the biggest one being when Louisa wanted to have a gap year and go travelling. It shocked her really how vehement her mum had been against it, she could normally get round her mum on most things but not that one. She'd grudgingly given in and agreed to go to uni, leaving the travelling until she'd qualified.

Diana ran her hands over Louisa's bedspread as some of these thoughts went round in her head. 'Oh Lou, you've repaid me a million times over. Look at what you've achieved through sheer hard work!' She sniffed hard, blew her nose and said to the mirror, 'Get a grip Diana, you've got to get on with it.' She picked up one of Louisa's baby photos. While she was gazing at it, something in it made her heart lurch. She started to become breathless. "Oh no, not again! Take long breaths, Di, in slowly through the nose, hold, out slowly through the mouth." Gradually, by talking herself through it, she managed to regulate her breathing. She looked back in the mirror. "What brought that on? You haven't had a panic attack for years, for goodness' sake!"

She got herself a glass of water and plonked down on the sofa. She reasoned that it was probably the stress of seeing Louisa off that had sparked the attack.

Louisa arrived in good time and without encountering any problems en route. Before she even got out of the car, she sent Diana a text.

Hi mum, here now. Will txt later luv u xx

She thought she would find out where her room was before she unloaded anything from the car and set off in the direction of the main entrance. She saw two girls in front and as she got nearer she said, "Excuse me, are you newbies too?"

"Oh hi! Yes we are. You too? Where are you heading?"

The three girls introduced themselves and set off to find their respective digs.

Diana wasn't entirely telling fibs when she told Louisa she had things planned. She had given it some thought and wondered if she might join something, or find some hobby. She had taken today off work to see Louisa off, thinking she probably wouldn't be able to concentrate anyway! To do something to keep her mind busy, she was looking online for anything that she might fancy joining, or doing, but nothing of any consequence really jumped out at her. She felt restless and fidgety, the panic attack had unnerved her. "Oh, I think I'll go for a walk and get some fresh air!"

She walked in the direction of the park. It was a fine day, quite warm really. She took the little footpath that cut through a small copse of trees. It was a curvy path, often used by joggers. Diana stopped and got closer to admire the shape of the leaves on one of the trees and as she turned to return to the path, she collided with a jogger who had just rounded a bend.

"Oh God, I'm so sorry! Are you okay?" The jogger was a woman of about her own age, Diana judged, fairly short with quite a rounded figure but obviously pretty fit.

"I'm fine thanks, no harm done, are you out for a stroll?"

"Yes, just getting some air. I'm sorry I've interrupted your run, I imagine you like to keep up a certain pace, sorry again."

The woman chuckled. Her voice was earthy and her laugh deep and throaty.

Diana smiled at her amusement, waiting for her to explain. "Believe me, you don't need to apologise to me for interrupting my run! I welcome any excuse to stop, and as for my pace... I don't think I have one! I'm no serious jogger!"

She introduced herself as Belinda.

"Can I ask why you run if you're not a serious jogger?" Diana asked.

"Simply because I promised my family I would, after I became so obese they were worried for my health," Belinda said, in a fairly matter-of-fact way.

"Oh God! I'm so sorry I shouldn't have pried, it's a bad habit of mine!"

"Oh please don't be sorry, it doesn't bother me to speak about it. I'm quite proud of myself since I lost two stone in weight but, although I really don't enjoy jogging, I know I have to keep up some sort of exercise, as well as follow my healthy diet, to not put it all back on and, as I said, I gave my word to my family. I knew they were worried about my health."

Diana admired the woman's honesty and commitment. They chatted a bit longer before Belinda said, "Oh well, can't put it off any longer! I'd better carry on, might bump into you again perhaps, enjoy your stroll!" And with that she was gone.

Their meeting gave Diana much food for thought. She hadn't told Belinda what her job was and an idea started to form in her head of how she could not only fill her time but make a difference at the same time. Back at the house, Diana opened up her laptop.

Louisa instantly liked Katy, a petite, blonde-haired girl and Emily, tall and willowy with gorgeous red hair. The two girls she had encountered on the way into the university were already friends. They came from the same town and had been at the same school, but seemed happy to let her join them as they went in search of their rooms. When Louisa found hers there was a girl already in the room next to hers, the door was open and she was sitting on the bed. Quite a plump, round-faced girl with short dark hair and wearing glasses. "Oh hi, I think we're neighbours, I'm Louisa," Louisa said brightly.

The girl looked up from what she was reading, gave Louisa an unsmiling glance and just about muttered "Hi".

With a heavy heart, Louisa went back to the car to start bringing her things up to the room. 'What a rude girl, she didn't even tell me what her name is!' she thought, as she stomped up the stairs.

Finally, Louisa got all her belongings up to her room – 'Hmm, I think I may have brought a bit too much stuff,' she admitted as she looked around the room. She couldn't even see the bed! She made a space and plonked herself down on it and suddenly felt very lonely. She resisted the temptation to pick up her mobile phone, knowing that if she did contact her mum she would immediately start worrying about her. 'Come on Loulou get a grip, you can do this,' she told herself and started trying to re-arrange her things in order to make better use of the meagre space.

Diana was so busy scrolling through the websites that Google had thrown up that she actually forgot to worry about Louisa for a little while! She wanted to research and glean as much information as possible before she made any attempts to put even a preliminary plan into action, but she definitely felt a sizzle of excitement. Who knew that from saying a teary goodbye to her lovely daughter this morning, a chance meeting with a stranger would result in her having an exciting, albeit tenuous at the moment, plan that might change her life!

She heard her tummy make grumblings of discontent and realised that she had been so engrossed with her research that she hadn't eaten any lunch. She closed the lid on her laptop and went to the kitchen to make herself a tuna salad, cutting off a huge chunk of bread to go with it, made herself a cup of coffee and it was then that her thoughts returned to Louisa. 'I wonder if she's settled in okay and what the other girls are like,' she pondered. Her thoughts flitted between Louisa and her research, her emotions alternating between concern and excitement. She didn't know why she had cut such a big chunk of bread as she really was having trouble swallowing bread. She pushed it to one side, picked about at the salad until she also pushed that away and reached for the biscuit tin, reasoning that dunked biscuits would be much easier to swallow.

When she judged that Louisa would have had time to settle into her room and, hopefully, made friends with someone on her floor, Diana sent a text, saying that she wasn't going to pester her but was just asking if she had got settled in okay. She was surprised to get a reply back almost instantly.

Hi mum, only just got my room straight. Met two nice girls, more later, luv u xx

'Typical Louisa, brief and to the point!' Diana thought, breathing a sigh of relief.

2

L ouisa was pleased her mum hadn't asked if her neighbour was nice! She thought she would make another attempt at conversation with the girl, reflecting that she was perhaps a bit anxious and shy and that had perhaps made her seem unfriendly. Louisa was always ready to see the good side of people.

The girl's door was now closed, so she gave it a tentative tap. There was no response, so she tapped a bit harder, wondering if the girl had gone exploring, something she was just about to do herself. Louisa was just about to walk away when the girl opened the door a little. "Oh hi again, sorry if you're in the middle of something, I just thought that, as we're neighbours and probably going to bump into each other quite a lot, it would be nice to just know each other's names. As I said mine is Louisa, what's yours?" Louisa said, feeling rather bold

The girl looked unsmilingly at Louisa. "Rosie."

Louisa thought this was going to be hard going. "Have you got all settled already, Rosie?" she asked.

"As settled as I can get," came the cryptic reply.

"Oh, have you got a problem with your room or something?"

"Only that I don't want to be in it!" came the sullen reply.

Louisa wondered whether she ought to just give this up as a bad job. She decided she would give up the polite approach anyway and just asked outright, "Why's that?"

She thought she saw a tear in the girl's eye as she loudly replied, "None of your effing business!" and slammed the door!

Diana was really cross with herself about not asking Belinda for her contact details when she'd spoken to her that morning. 'Still', she reasoned, 'I know she regularly jogs there, I can probably catch her one morning before I go to work.'

She wanted to speak to Belinda to sound her out before getting any deeper into her research. Her work as a counsellor would be good grounding for the change in direction, she thought, but she really needed to do much more research. There was a lot to it and a lot to think about, it would be a huge step to take.

After several attempts, Diana finally bumped into Belinda one morning when one of her appointments had cancelled at the last minute. Fortunately it was a fine day, giving her the opportunity to go for a walk.

"Hi Belinda, I was hoping I would bump into you, I totally forgot to ask you any details of where you live, phone number etc. and, after our meeting I really rather wanted to have a little chat with you about something if it would be okay?"

"I thought exactly the same! About the details that is, not about you wanting to chat to me!" Belinda laughed. "Shall I put my number in your phone?"

"Oh! That's a good idea!" Diana said, as she handed her

mobile phone over. They discovered that Belinda only lived a few streets away from the cul-de-sac where Diana now lived and they arranged that Diana would call round to her on Friday evening.

"Paul spends a couple of hours at the gym after work on Fridays, his wind-down time after a week at work, and the girls both have things planned so we can have a chat without being disturbed," Belinda explained.

"How old are the girls?" Diana asked.

"Paige is 25 and Saffron is 27," Belinda replied.

"Wow! You don't look old enough to have children that age!" Diana exclaimed, thinking that Belinda must be quite a bit older than her. "They're both still at home, then?"

"Oh thanks! Yes they are, although I think Saffron will soon be moving in with her fiancé. They've been saving up for a place so it made sense for them to each stay living with their parents until they have enough, a lot cheaper living with mum and dad!" Belinda said with a grin.

Diana liked her, and her sense of humour

Diana found Belinda's house easily and rung the doorbell, when Belinda threw open the door with a smiling "Hi Diana!" She was met with a delicious smell of something baking. The hall was a wonderful, casual, muddle of coats, shoes and bags, some of which were balanced precariously on top of an ageing dresser and struggling for space with a bowl which had loads of keys in it, an untidy heap of papers and, smiling through the lot, a large ornament of a spotted cow, the huge grin on its face looking at one and the same time both ridiculous and endearing. Diana immediately felt the warmth of this home.

"Something smells delicious!" she said, as she followed Belinda through the hall and into the kitchen.

"I've just been baking some of Paul's favourite muffins. The girls will be here during the morning tomorrow so they'll all make short work of them between them! Would you like one with a coffee? Or would a glass of wine go down better? I thought we'd sit in the conservatory, is that okay," she finished, putting a baking tin away and went back into the hall and through to the lounge, indicating the conservatory beyond. Diana followed her, smiling to herself at the way Belinda hadn't come up for breath long enough for her to reply to the first question before she went into the second.

The smell of the muffins was too tempting to refuse. "Errm well a coffee and a muffin sounds lovely please, Belinda, they do smell so delicious and the conservatory looks a lovely relaxing place to sit."

"Make yourself comfortable then, I won't be long. I've got some fresh coffee brewed," Belinda said, as she ambled back out to the kitchen, calling over her shoulder, "Do you take milk and sugar?"

"Neither thank you," Diana replied as she removed some magazines from an armchair and sunk into the soft, well worn cushions. She could already tell she and Belinda would become firm friends, and a good friend was something she was missing in her life right now.

"So what did you want to chat about?" Belinda asked, once they were settled in the conservatory with their coffee and muffins, Belinda explaining she allowed herself one treat a day! "Well, after chatting to you the first time we met, when you said your family had given you a wake-up call about your health, I had an idea for a change of direction for myself."

"Well, you don't need to worry about your weight, you have a wonderful figure," Belinda interjected.

"No, no I wasn't meaning about how I see myself, thank you by the way! But more how I could be of help to others."

Belinda looked puzzled.

"I'm thinking about training to be a life coach. I'm currently a counsellor, I thought it might be a good grounding for it. It might be a crazy idea but I thought about how your family had helped you make a conscious decision concerning how you live your life in order to be healthier and the idea was formed. What do you think? Would it have helped you to have had a life coach, do you think?"

"What made you decide to become a counsellor?" Belinda asked, munching on her muffin.

Diana shifted in her chair. "My mother died before I was going to start university. I was going to be late starting, I'd had a gap year and it was a complete shock when mum became ill and subsequently passed away. It was a difficult time and the counselling sessions I had at the time were invaluable. I still see a counsellor on odd occasions. They really helped me to eventually get back on track so I decided I would train to be one too and hopefully help others in the same way." She had a sip of her coffee.

"Oh I'm so sorry about your mum. What about your dad?"

"Dad found it hard of course for quite a while, but he is a strong, stoical character and he was a great support to me. I should have been supporting him, really," she ended rather wistfully as her voice drifted off. She shook herself out of the moment. "These muffins are delicious by the way!" she said with enthusiasm.

"Glad you're enjoying it and in answer to your question, I've never really thought about what a life coach does before really but, yes, thinking about it now I guess it would have been quite helpful."

They both enjoyed the couple of hours and arranged to meet for coffee in town the following Saturday. "We've got a family day this Saturday, the girls are here in the morning and Paul and I are going shopping together in the afternoon, a rarity I can tell you! But he promised me we could look for something for Saffy and Tom for their new home!"

"That's absolutely fine with me, I'll look forward to it," Diana said, as she picked up her handbag to leave. At the door, she turned and gave Belinda a hug. "Thank you for a lovely chat, *and* a delicious muffin! I'm so pleased we met."

"So am I. Fate must have brought you to this town!"

"Well, it was the university location actually, but I know what you mean!" Diana laughingly replied.

Louisa soon settled into university life and was determined to study hard. She wanted to be a doctor and knew that meant hard work. However, she also liked the social side of the life and often went out with Katy and Emily. She still tried to make friends with Rosie. On one occasion, she tapped her door and offered her some of the biscuits her mum had sent in a parcel of other goodies. *Just a few things you might be missing* the note had said, which made Louisa feel a little bit homesick.

Rosie was her usual curt self. "Why do you keep trying to make friends with me?" she asked. Louisa often asked herself that question and she could never answer it. She just felt she needed to.

"Why not?" Louisa replied. "Take them they're not poisonous, although they are home-made I can assure you my mum wouldn't put anything dodgy in them. Here, just take them. It's up to you whether you eat them or not," she said with a shrug, thrusting them into the girl's arms.

Despite herself, Rosie took them and gave a muttered, "Thank you". Progress had been made!

3

NINETEEN YEARS EARLIER

As soon as she walked out of the door of the plane onto the platform at the top of the flight steps, she felt the heat envelop her like a warm blanket and, as she descended, each step brought her nearer to her adventure. She was filled with excited anticipation and a not too small amount of anxiety.

'This is it, I'm here and on my way,' she thought, as she strode purposefully towards the arrivals entrance with a confidence she really didn't feel.

When this opportunity had presented itself to her, she had pondered long and hard before making the decision to come. Her parents, though she knew they were somewhat hesitant and not at all sure that it was the right thing to do, were quite modern thinking and, as always, supportive so they had allowed her to delay going to university for a year when she saw the advert for an au pair in the agency she frequently browsed looking for a Saturday job. She was allowed to spend some of the money left to her by her Gran to pay for the flight. They insisted on buying her a mobile phone, "Just in case of emergencies." There was a teary goodbye at the airport, a check to ensure she had everything, including the mobile phone! "Make sure you keep in touch!" her mum shouted as she went through the barrier.

The ant-like procession of disembarked passengers snaked its way onwards. She kept them in sight until she had successfully passed through border control and baggage reclamation. As she entered the arrival lounge, she scanned the awaiting crowd for anyone holding a placard with her name on it. With each second, her anxiety rose. 'What if nobody comes for me?' she asked herself, then her stomach gave a lurch as she saw a small man pop out from behind a huge pillar holding up a board with her name on it. As the flight landed at night, she had pre-booked an overnight stay in a nearby hotel which had a pick-up service. She made her way a little anxiously to the little man, confirmed that she was who he was waiting for and was soon being whisked to her hotel.

As soon as she was in her hotel room, as instructed by her mum, she rang to say she had arrived safely. She had a surprisingly good night's sleep and after a different, but totally delicious, breakfast she positioned herself, with her luggage, in the foyer to wait for whoever it was that was going to come for her. The longer she waited, the more anxious she got. It felt as though she had been waiting for hours but, in fact, when, finally, a small, dark-haired man came towards her with his white teeth smiling a welcome, it was only fifteen minutes since she'd sat down. Her stomach gave a lurch. 'Definitely no going back now!' she told herself.

The house they arrived at was huge and more modern than she had envisaged. The little man opened the car door for her and after he'd got her luggage from the boot he gestured for her to go ahead of him up the curved stone steps. She waited at the door, he opened it and waved her in. She let out a gasp as she gazed in awe at the beauty of the entrance hall in which they stood.

She snapped her head round as she heard footsteps. "Ahh! I see that you have arrived safely. It's Diana, isn't it?" The woman who approached was petite, beautifully dressed and spoke with a very soft voice.

"Yes, Diana."

A very attractive woman with kind, almond-shaped eyes, she smiled as she held out her hand. "I'm so pleased to meet you, Diana. Brinal will show you to your quarters. Please take your time to settle yourself and come down when you're ready and I will take you to meet the children."

Diana shook the hand proffered, nervously saying, "I'm very pleased to meet you too Madam, thank you."

"Oh please, call me Hiruni!" Diana felt more relaxed.

It wasn't long before she was stood gazing in amazement around the bedroom. "Wow, it's huge!" she said with a gasp. The room was more a bedsit than a bedroom as, besides the very sumptuous looking bed, there was a large upholstered armchair, an ornate small table with chair to match and its own luxurious en-suite bathroom! She plonked herself down on the bed, puffing out her cheeks and letting out a huge puff of breath. She couldn't stop gazing around the room. "I'm actually here, I'm actually doing this!"

She took out the mobile phone she was still learning how to use. Her parents had bought themselves one too especially so that they could keep in contact with her. She wanted to send them a quick text to let them know she had arrived safely, but when she tried it wouldn't go.

She wandered over to the window. Her room was at the back of the house, overlooking the huge expanse of manicured gardens. As she admired the view and marvelled at the colours, she saw a movement out of the corner of her eye. Someone was meandering down a long, winding, paved pathway which ran between two full mixed borders of the most beautiful flowers. It was a man, he stopped and reached forwards towards a big clump of fiery red flowers. When he stood up she could see that he had picked one of the flowers and, as he held it up to his nose he turned and looked straight up at her window! Diana quickly ducked out of sight. Although he was quite a way away, there had been something in the way he had looked up that had sent a shiver down her spine.

She jumped at the knock on her door. When she opened it, Brinal was there. "Madam asks if you ready, come to meet children please."

She smiled at him. "Thank you Brinal, shall I follow you?" His face broke into a huge smile, he was obviously pleased that she had not only remembered his name but had used it! He nodded, she followed him until they met Hiruni at the bottom of the first flight of stairs.

"This way, the children are in the playroom," she said. Brinal left them as Diana followed Hiruni along the corridor. They passed two doors on the right and one on the left before they stopped at another on the left. There was a key in the lock, which Hiruni turned.

"They're locked in?!" Diana said without thinking.

Hiruni's kind eyes now held a steely glint but her voice was smooth and quiet. "The children's safety is of the utmost importance. That is something you must never forget whilst they are in your charge. They must never be allowed to wander about outside unaccompanied, I trust you will remember that?"

"Yes, of course," Diana replied with a sinking heart. 'Whatever have I done coming here?' she thought. She had serious misgivings and she hadn't even met the children yet!

Hiruni threw open the door. "Mami! Mami!" The two children ran to her. The boy seemed shy when he saw Diana.

She knew from the information she had received that he was the youngest at six years old. The girl, she also knew, was nine years old, and she could see was considerably more confident than her little brother.

"Children, this is Miss Diana."

"Are you our new au pair?" said the girl in perfect English.

"Hello, yes I am. What's your name?"

"Eshani."

"That's a pretty name, and what about you, little man, what shall I call you?" Diana bent down to the little boy.

"Ashan," he whispered.

"Ashan, you must speak up so that Miss Diana can hear you!" his mother said.

Diana felt sorry for the little lad. "Actually, I have really wonderful hearing Ashan, and sometimes I can hear even the smallest whisper, aren't I lucky?" she said. He gave a shy smile but when Diana looked up at Hiruni, expecting her to be pleased that she had won her son's confidence, it was not pleasure she saw in her eyes!

"You will take your meals during the day – that is, breakfast and lunch – with the children in the small breakfast room off of the kitchen and sometimes may have to do so with your evening meal, depending on what social arrangements we have made. Otherwise, you may eat with the rest of the family. The children will have tea at 5pm, cook will serve breakfast at 8am and lunch at 12.30. You will take the children to school after breakfast and collect them for lunch and return them to school after. Is that quite clear to you?" Although Hiruni said all this to Diana in the same calm voice she had used earlier, Diana felt a sense of foreboding.

"Yes, perfectly clear thank you," she said in a more clipped fashion than she'd intended. "Is the school very far away?" she added.

"Not at all," was the terse reply.

All the while this exchange was taking place, the two children sat on their chairs at a table that had books, paints and other crafting items on it, without once moving or interrupting. Diana thought that they were either very well behaved, or it was as she sensed, that they had gone through this ritual before and were used to the format!

"Now children, perhaps you could show Miss Diana around the house. You have time before cook serves lunch," and with that Hiruni glided out of the room.

Eshani was a very good guide. Again Diana thought she seemed well practised in the art. "Have you had many au pairs?" she asked in a chatty fashion.

"Quite a lot, I can't remember how many," the little girl replied. Diana wondered why there was such a turnover of them but put the thought to the back of her mind as she gently took hold of Ashan's hand. He was confident enough to leave it there, which pleased her.

The day passed very quickly as she entertained the children, joined them for their lunch and watched over them as they ate their tea. Hiruni hadn't explained to her what happened about their bedtime so she tried to quietly ask cook when she brought in their tea but the language barrier made it difficult. She had to resort to asking Eshani.

"Mami comes to find us after tea," was the reply.

Sure enough, at 6.30pm, Hiruni came and found them. "Have you had a good day?" she asked, her gaze encompassing both the children and Diana. The children excitedly told her all that they had done with Diana and as it seemed to meet with Hiruni's approval, Diana breathed a sigh of relief. Hiruni turned to her, saying, "I shall take the children from you now. You will be eating with the family this evening so would you get changed into suitable attire and join us in the big dining room at 8pm." This said as she took in Diana's clothing with a sweeping glance!

~

"Suitable attire?" Diana mouthed to herself in the mirror when in her room. She had a leisurely soak in the bath and pondered on her day, after which she wrote in the diary she had started before she left England. She scanned the clothes that she had hung in the wardrobe, puzzling what would be deemed 'suitable attire' and settled on a white cotton blouse to wear with the navy blue version of the two new, long, linen skirts she had treated herself to. It passed her inspection, she just hoped it would pass Hiruni's!

She left her room and walked down the corridor but at the end she got disorientated and couldn't remember which way to go. As she was deliberating a tall, dark, rather good looking, man came towards her. "Are you lost?" he asked in perfect English.

"Yes, I've forgotten which way to go for the dining room," she said shyly.

"Well, that's just where I'm going so you can walk with me. My wife tells me you are looking after our children. Remind me of your name, I'm sorry I'm not good with names."

"Diana," she felt quite out of her depth. She was okay with the children but she wasn't used to making small talk with strangers.

"I'm pleased to meet you, Diana. I am Ravan. Ahh here we are, in you go," he said, opening the door for her.

The room was very formal and very ornate. Hiruni was

standing over the other side of the huge table and standing by the long window at the other side of the room was the man Diana had seen from her window.

"Oh, I see you have met my husband, Diana. This is my brother Suresh, Suresh this is Diana the new au pair for the children." He came slowly towards her and Diana felt embarrassed and shy as his dark gaze swept over her.

"How lovely!" he said as he took her hand.

Diana swallowed and whispered, "Hello".

"Suresh! Let the girl get to the table!" Hiruni said crossly.

4

Throughout the meal, Diana could feel his eyes on her. It unnerved her, she already felt shy sitting at a table with strangers. She privately hoped she would not have to eat with them very often. She was suddenly very pleased that her parents had made her buy an open-ended return air ticket!

The next morning, after a disturbed night's sleep of weird dreams, she made her way to find the children in the breakfast room. She was surprised and somewhat shaken to see Suresh there.

"Good morning lovely Diana!" he said as he stood watching her go to the children.

"Good morning. Hello you two, you've beaten me!" she said lightly, avoiding Suresh's eyes and seating herself at the table next to Ashan.

"We have to be here by 8 o'clock," Eshani told her. "So, actually, you are late."

Diana's heart sank. No doubt Suresh would report to his sister.

Suresh smiled to himself with amusement. "Well, I'll leave you all to your breakfast. Have a good day," he said with a chuckle.

Despite thoughts of flying home, Diana decided to give it a bit longer and over the weeks that followed found herself becoming attached to the children. She even became used to Suresh turning up wherever she was. If she was in the garden with the children, he was suddenly sitting on a bench. When she dropped the children off at school, there he was on the other side of the road. Fortunately, when she decided to wander around the town on her own, which she often did, she didn't see him but, even when she was just walking down one of the hallways in the house, he just appeared from nowhere.

She wondered why he was always about, why he didn't seem to do any work, so when she had the opportunity she asked Brinal. She found him in the kitchen talking to cook. "Hello Brinal."

He came towards her. "Miss Diana," he said, inclining his head.

"Can I ask you something?" He nodded. "What does Suresh do? Does he not go to work? He always seems to be around."

"His work is here, Miss Diana. He must be sure the children are safe."

"But I thought that was why I was here!" Diana said.

"You are here to amuse the children, not keep them safe," he replied quietly.

Diana felt a tightness in her chest! All this talk of safety was making her nervous. It didn't help that there was no signal here for her to use her mobile phone, either.

As soon as she went through the arch into the back garden she regretted it, as there was Suresh. He must have got back earlier than normal from his patrol of the outside of the school, which she now knew he did after she had dropped off the children.

"Ahh Miss Diana, are you looking for me?"

"Err no, actually I was looking for Brinal. Not to worry, I'll find him later," she said and turned to retrace her steps back through the arch.

"Perhaps I can help you?" he ventured.

Diana hesitated. She supposed she could ask him what she was going to ask Brinal. She turned back again to face him and tentatively said, "Before I decided to come here I did a bit of research."

"That's very sensible," he interrupted.

She didn't respond but continued with her speech before she lost the courage to do so. "I know there was a war here a few years ago but I thought it was all over long ago. My parents wouldn't have let me come if there was still trouble, so I wondered why it is that there is always talk of keeping the children safe." She expelled her breath loudly, relieved to have got the words out.

He came closer. Her heart beat faster, but he quietly said, "You are quite correct about the war. However, in some areas not too far from here there are still some violent clashes. Some schools are not even open because of danger to the children. We are lucky here and you are quite safe. However, my sister and brother-in-law worry very much about my niece and nephew, as they remember the awful times in the war, hence the constant vigilance for their safety."

Diana swallowed hard.

"Does that answer your question?" Suresh asked.

"Yes, thank you," she said and turned to go.

"I'll walk you back to the house," he said, putting his hand under her elbow. Diana stiffened. She didn't think he was allowed to touch her, her heart rate quickened. "Don't be nervous little girl, I mean you no harm. You will see that it is not me you need to be nervous about," and with that he left her side and walked around the back of the house.

It left Diana shaken. 'What did he mean, not him? Does he mean I have to be nervous of someone else?' she asked herself.

Life seemed to settle down okay after that. Although Diana was still a bit nervous of Suresh, nothing else was mentioned about their conversation. She occasionally saw Ravan. He was always very pleasant to her, asked her how her day had been, how the children were behaving, if she was happy there and was generally very nice. He and Hiruni spent some time together with the children but only at certain times of the day. Diana felt quite sorry for her charges. She found the different culture quite strange in comparison with her own childhood.

'Still, I wouldn't have the job if it wasn't like this,' she told herself. She said all this to her parents when she was able to ring them from the town.

One day after a few months of her being there, while the children were at school, Brinal found her and said the mistress was waiting in the garden for her. Diana wondered what she had done wrong.

"I'm afraid I have some bad news for you, Diana."

Diana's heart jumped into her throat. "What's wrong?" she asked.

"I have had a message from the agency. I'm afraid your mother isn't very well. It seems you must return home."

Diana's heart raced. "My mum? What's wrong with her?"

"I'm afraid I don't know the details but it seems as though it's serious enough for you to return home."

Diana felt sick. "I don't understand, she was fine when I spoke to her a couple of days ago!"

"Yes, well, it is very sudden and I can understand your upset. It is unfortunate for you and isn't entirely convenient timing for me either as Brinal has to return to his parents for a few days for a family matter and with you leaving it means that Suresh will have to look after the children as I have several appointments to attend."

Although this was said in Hiruni's normal soft voice, the annoyance wasn't lost on Diana and she couldn't help but retaliate. "Well, I'm very sorry that my mother's ill health has come at an inconvenient time," she said hotly. "I have an open-ended ticket and will leave on the first available flight!" she added, with tears in her eyes.

Hiruni bristled at the girl's tone but her anguish wasn't lost on her. She had actually become quite fond of Diana and felt uncharacteristically empathetic towards her at this moment so, instead of berating her for her tone, she said, "I will make all your travel arrangements. I know there is a flight tomorrow morning. You will have to go to the hotel this evening though as none of us will be available to take you in the morning. I will book you a room. As my husband is the only one who is available this evening, I will ask him to take you. I am sorry that you have this worry about your mother."

Diana was quite taken aback. Although Hiruni had always been polite and not really unkind to her, she had always been somewhat aloof and this was probably the first time she had used kind words to her. "Thank you, I will go and get my things packed," she replied, still with tears in her eyes.

Brinal came to say goodbye before he left for his parents'

home and she had time to say goodbye to the children before their bedtime. She would miss them, there were tears as she hugged them on the steps. Suresh came to say goodbye! He had a concerned look in his eye.

"Be careful little girl," he said, as he shook her hand.

Even Hiruni shook her hand and said, "I hope everything turns out okay for your mother."

Ravan put her luggage in the boot and they left for the hotel. When they arrived, he carried her luggage to the reception desk, even though she had protested, saying "You don't have to do that!"

"Of course I will, it's the least I can do," he smilingly said. "Right, let us get you booked into your room."

5

PRESENT DAY

Diana and Louisa had regular news swaps on the phone. "Alex keeps asking how you're doing Lou, have you not contacted him since you left?"

Alex was a friend of Louisa's who really wanted to be more than just a friend.

"He's a nice boy, Lou," Diana often said but was aware that she had to let Louisa choose her own boyfriend!

"I know he is mum, I like him a lot, but only as a friend."

Louisa kept plodding away at trying to gain Rosie's confidence and gradually, bit by bit, she actually got her to come into her room for a 'girlie' evening, just the two of them. She thought it might be pushing it a bit to invite Katy and Emily for the first time. As it was, Rosie had only very grudgingly accepted.

Halfway through the evening, and the illicit bottle of vodka they were sharing, Rosie began to loosen a little and began to open up to Louisa. Even though Louisa was adopted, she had a similar way of being able to relax people as Diana did.

"My dad died six months before uni started," Rosie said in a faraway voice.

Louisa realised that she had to reply to that information very carefully. "I'm sorry, that must have been very tough for you and your mum," she said quietly. "It was brave of both of you for you to still come," she continued.

For a minute Rosie's eyes flared and Louisa thought she had got her approach wrong, but they subsided again and Rosie said, "Not brave on my part, I fought like bloody hell with my mum about coming, I just didn't want to be here. At the time I just couldn't see the point in coming, couldn't see the point in anything really and, of course, my mum was grieving, I sometimes thought she just wanted me to be away from her so that she could grieve in peace!"

"Oh Rosie, she would never have thought that!"

As they continued to chat, Louisa found out that it was Rosie's uncle, her dad's brother, who had finally persuaded her to come. He had even brought her. "I think he wanted to make sure I didn't do a runner!" she said. "My dad was a police sergeant and because of his job and the way he always said 'It's alright me catching the villains but it's what happens afterwards!' that I decided to become a lawyer, so that I can help to see that justice is done. Dad was thrilled with my decision."

"Well, I think your dad would be so proud, Rosie, and you can't give up on it now. However you feel about being here, you would be letting down your dad!"

It gave Rosie much food for thought the next morning in the sober, cold light of day. After that she began to concentrate more on her studies. She still had days when she was sulky and somewhat morose, but Louisa now knew those days and knew how to deal with Rosie when they happened.

Another time when they were having a heart to heart,

Louisa tentatively asked how Rosie's dad had died. She wondered privately if it was to do with his work. "Don't answer if you don't want to talk about it," she added.

"It's okay, I can now, he had an aneurysm. It was a total shock as he'd never had any sign of illness and was really fit, passed all his work check-ups! He was actually out jogging when he had it. By the time someone saw him and called the ambulance, it was too late!"

"Wow, I'm so sorry, that must have been awful for you and your mum!"

"I'm afraid mum didn't deal with it very well." She paused, looked as though she was deciding whether to go into more detail or not and obviously made the decision to do so. Louisa saw the conflict playing out in her face and just waited. Eventually, Rosie continued, "I didn't tell you before, I don't generally tell anyone, I don't like to talk about it, but mum is an alcoholic now. Please don't judge her, or be sympathetic to me!" she finished hotly.

Louisa was at a loss to know what to say so just said, "I wouldn't judge anyone, Rosie, without knowing their story." Then as an afterthought she said, "I have never known a dad," hoping it would change the direction of Rosie's thoughts. It did. Rosie apologised for always taking over the conversation with her own problems and asked Louisa to tell her more.

She told Rosie she was adopted and why there was only her and her mum.

"Have you never wanted to find your birth parents?" Rosie asked.

"No, not really, my mum and I are very close and she's worked really hard to give me everything she could. I wouldn't want to hurt her, but I must admit I am sometimes curious, and have got more curious recently. As you can see I'm not white, so I must have some foreign blood in me somewhere. Mum says they didn't ask any details, they just fell in love with me and that was that!"

"Has your mum never had any boyfriends?"

"Yes, she has had a few, some quite nice, some decidedly not! But they never seemed to last."

"Don't you feel angry that your birth parents gave you up?"

"As I said before, Rosie, I don't judge anyone without knowing the story. Anyway, far from being angry I feel thankful that my mum and dad chose me! Albeit that he flew the coop before the deed was done! I have always been sad though that I have never known a dad, I must admit."

Completely out of character for her, Rosie suddenly gave Louisa a hug. It shook Louisa, but not as much as the unfamiliar feeling she had in her groin! She jerked away from Rosie in shock.

"What's wrong? Sorry, that was an impulse. I didn't mean to scare you!" Rosie said, herself rather shaken at her impulsive gesture. She looked up at Louisa's face, studied it, she loved her almond-shaped eyes, her lips were finely shaped and suddenly she just had an urge to kiss them!

Louisa caught her look. They sat there looking at each other both struggling to understand what had just happened between them. "I... I errm, I'd better get back to some studying," Louisa eventually said and hurried out.

Things became a little awkward with them for a while after that. Neither one of them knew quite how to react to the other. Louisa had previously, after speaking to her mum about it, invited Rosie to come home with her for the upcoming Christmas holiday, knowing that she only had her uncle to stay with, as her mum was in rehab "Again!" Rosie had exclaimed.

Privately, Louisa had thought that her mum could perhaps use some of her counselling skills to help Rosie in some way. Rosie's uncle had okayed it. The break was looming ever closer and Louisa wasn't sure what to do about it now. Ever the practical one, she made a decision and knocked on Rosie's door, saying when Rosie opened the door, "Can we talk?"

"Yes, I think we should, come in."

Louisa sat on the edge of Rosie's bed. "Something happened between us, didn't it?" she boldly said. "I know you felt it too."

"Yes, I did, I actually wanted to kiss you," Rosie ventured.

"Really?! Do you still want to?"

"Yes," Rosie replied, plonking herself down next to Louisa. She held her hand, they looked at each other and slowly Rosie leaned in to Louisa. They tentatively found each other's lips, broke slowly away, eyes searching each other's face and kissed again, this time more fervently. They released each other, looked at each other, then hugged tightly.

Louisa whispered in Rosie's ear, "I haven't felt like this before."

Rosie held her away from her and saw tears slowly rolling down her cheeks. "Is this the first time you've kissed another girl?"

"Yes, I think I'm only just working out who I am. Have you had other girlfriends? In this way, I mean."

"Only one, it didn't last. Just a couple of kids fumbling about really, but I've always known that I wasn't interested in boys and knew from about thirteen that I was probably a lesbian."

"Oh – what about your parents? Do they know, sorry, I mean did your dad and does your mum?"

"Dad did and he was brilliant. Somehow I could never tell mum and now she has too much going on in her head!"

Louisa wondered how her mum would take the news when she eventually told her, as she would need to, because she was now sure of her sexuality. It answered a lot of questions for her.

6

Diana was beside herself with excitement about Louisa being home for Christmas and, as her father was going to be spending Christmas in New Zealand with her brother and his family, had planned all sorts of things for the two of them to do. She was, if she was honest, a little bit disappointed when Lou had asked her if she could bring home her friend Rosie, she didn't want to share her, but of course when she heard Rosie's story she couldn't refuse.

'My girl is growing up and independent, I can't have her all to myself forever,' she told herself.

She hadn't seen much of Belinda of late as she had been busy dividing her time between her work, her research and the Christmas preparations. Belinda was busy too doing the same for a big family Christmas. But they had made time to meet up today. She couldn't wait to tell Louisa that she had enrolled herself into a life-coach course starting after the Christmas break!

As the car pulled up, Diana ran down to greet them. She threw her arms around Louisa. "Oh it's so lovely to see you, darling, have you lost weight? Oh your hair's grown! You look happy!"

Louisa laughed at her mum's quick-fire chat. "Lovely to see you too, mum! This is Rosie."

"Oh Rosie I'm sorry, I didn't mean to ignore you! Hello I'm so pleased to meet you." She wrapped Rosie in a hug. Rosie stiffened a little but stayed in the brief hug and as Diana released her said, "I'm pleased to meet you too, Mrs—"

"—Oh please call me Diana!"

"Thank you for letting me come, Diana," Rosie smiled.

"You're more than welcome. Come on, let's get your things inside."

By the evening they were all three munching on sausage rolls and Christmas cookies, enjoying a drink, playing a board game and laughing hysterically.

Louisa had thought more and more about finding out about her birth parents but she couldn't bring herself to tell her mum that she wanted to do so. Rosie asked her if she had seen if there was a name on her adoption certificate.

"I haven't got my adoption certificate. Every time I've needed it my mum has dealt with whatever I've needed it for." Louisa decided she would ask her mum for it, saying she needed it for something at uni.

Diana noticed the closeness between her daughter and Rosie and it dawned on her that this may be more than just the special bond of friends. She had seen all sorts of clients in her work and dealt with all sorts of relationships. She was sure that her beloved girl had discovered her own sexuality but would wait until she felt ready to discuss it, as she was sure she would.

So, when Louisa found her in the kitchen, putting the

finishing touches to the Christmas supper (even though they had all said they didn't think they could eat another thing after the huge Christmas dinner they'd eaten!) Diana felt sure that she was going to tell her. "Mum?"

"Yes my darling?" Diana had prepared what she would say and was ready.

"Could I have my adoption certificate? I need it for something I'm working on in one of my studies."

The knife clattering to the floor made them both jump. "Are you okay, mum?" Louisa could see her mum was starting to do her breathing exercises.

"I'll... be okay... in a minute... darling," Diana said between breaths. Louisa thought her mum had guessed why she wanted the adoption certificate and it had caused one of her panic attacks. She didn't pursue the subject further and thought she'd better not tell her yet about her and Rosie!

She had asked her mum, while Rosie was in the shower, "What do you think of Rosie, mum?"

Diana thought out her answer carefully before replying, having thought that Rosie probably was, at this moment in time, quite special to Louisa. "I think she's very nice darling, a little troubled maybe, which isn't surprising as she's dealing with her grief and worrying about her mum, but she seems quite a strong character so, with support, I'm sure she'll come out the other side."

When Diana had a moment alone with Louisa, she told her of her plan to become a life coach. "Mum, that's brilliant! You'll be really good at that!"

"I hope so, but I would like to give it a go, something I think I can apply myself to."

A couple of days before they were due to leave, Louisa summoned up the courage to have a chat to her mum. She wanted her to know about her and Rosie before they went back to uni.

"Mum?"

Diana stiffened, expecting Louisa to mention the adoption certificate again.

"Yes Lou Lou?"

"I have something to tell you, about me. I've been wanting to tell you ever since we arrived but haven't found the right moment. I want to tell you before we go back."

"Would this be anything to do with you and Rosie, darling?"

"You knew, mum?!"

"Well, I guessed, Lou."

"Oh mum, I've been stewing on it ever since we arrived! Are you okay about me being gay?"

"My darling girl, I couldn't care less what you are as long as you're happy. All I will worry about is that whoever you fall in love with doesn't hurt you! Just be careful to not fall too deeply too soon. Rosie is dealing with a lot at the moment, which will affect her emotions in many ways."

"Don't worry, mum. I'll be okay." Louisa gave her mum a huge hug.

"I love you, Lou Lou."

"Love you too, mum."

7

A few weeks after they were back at uni, Rosie put the idea to Louisa that she could get her own copy of her adoption certificate. "You can say you've lost the original, I'm sure you can ask for another."

Louisa found all the details on the website, completed the application and paid the amount due. She felt a little frisson of excitement to be taking this first step on her quest, but also a little guilty, as if she was betraying her mum.

Each day, Louisa checked to see if there was any post for her.

"You've got to give it time!" Rosie said.

"I know, I wonder how long it will take?"

Finally, she had an official looking letter. She ran to Rosie's room, waving it in the air. "I think this is it!" she exclaimed. They sat on the bed together.

"Go on then, open it!" Rosie urged.

With shaking hands, Louisa opened it. "There's just a letter!"

"What does it say?"

"It says they have no record of an adoption certificate for me!"

~

Excited to be finding a new direction, Diana found her evening courses fascinating.

"It's interesting, isn't it?" She hadn't heard him come up behind her, while ordering her coffee in the little coffee bar around the corner from the college, where she'd got into the habit of popping into before going home. She jumped and as she turned she recognised him as a fellow student.

"Sorry, I didn't mean to startle you! I recognised you from the course."

She had seen him there and had thought he was quite a pleasant looking man. "You just made me jump. I didn't hear you come up behind me but yes, in answer to your question, it is very interesting."

He smiled, she liked his smile. "Can I join you?"

She hesitated for a second, her pulse quickened, a voice in her head said, 'For goodness sake, it's just a coffee!' then out loud she said, "Yes, of course."

Diana found him easy to talk to, discovered his name was Mark, that he had been married once and amicably divorced, no children. When Diana asked him what had made him join this course, he said he had been made redundant from a high-flying job with an American company a few months ago.

"I floundered a bit, I was like a fish out of water after doing a high-powered job, got a bit depressed if I'm honest. A mate suggested I make an appointment with a life coach he knew, it helped me enormously, so much so that I thought it would be something I could have a go at, a new interest. What about you?"

Diana told him briefly why she was on the course. Then they spoke about past relationships.

"I've been on my own for about six years now," Mark said. "I've had a few dates from online dating sites, but nothing really worked out."

Diana told him that she had one adopted daughter and no man in her life. She didn't even feel embarrassed to speak about it with him, as she usually did!

"Wow look at the time!" Diana exclaimed. "I didn't realise it was that late, I'd better go. Thank you for the coffee, I've enjoyed chatting with you."

"I have thoroughly enjoyed myself, Diana. I wonder, would you fancy having a meal sometime?"

She surprised herself by replying without hesitation. "I'd like that, yes." They exchanged phone numbers.

As they got outside, Mark leaned forward and pecked her on the cheek. "See you soon," he said. "I'll ring you."

"Okay!" she smiled and found herself smiling during most of the drive home! Her phone rang as she opened her front door.

"Why not make it this Saturday?" Mark began, without even saying hello.

Diana smiled to herself. "Why not indeed!" she said.

8

NINETEEN YEARS EARLIER

Diana felt sick, she threw herself on her bed and sobbed. Her mum was right, she *was* frightened, she'd felt frightened and upset all the way home! She had no idea her mum was so ill, she didn't know what to say to her, or her dad. Finally she controlled her sobs, went to the bathroom and washed her face and steeled herself to go back downstairs.

As she went into the lounge her mum, resting on the sofa, held out her arms to her. "Come here angel," she said softly.

Diana sat down heavily next to her and threw her arms around her mum's neck. "I'm sorry for what I said, mum," she said into her mum's shoulder, as she started to cry again.

"It's alright darling, I know it was a shock to see me so poorly but in all honesty I really wasn't this poorly when we last spoke. I didn't say anything then as I was sure it was just something that would pass and saw no point in worrying you needlessly. I wasn't to know that it was more than that."

Diana's dad came across the room. She looked round and

saw tears in his eyes, she stood up and hugged him. "Sorry dad," she whispered. He stroked her head and kissed it.

Later when she and her dad were in the kitchen, she asked quietly, "Dad? Is mum going to die?" She saw his shoulders shake as he quietly sobbed and knew the answer.

Diana's older brother Steven flew back from New Zealand a few weeks later, which turned out to be just a few days before she passed away. At the funeral he worried about his dad, but he could also see that Diana really wasn't well at all. "Sis, are you okay?"

"Of course I'm not okay," she snapped and walked outside.

He followed her. "Sis wait. I didn't mean just today. You look ill, have you seen a doctor since you got back? I know it's been a lot for you to process and don't bite my head off but I really think perhaps you ought to see a counsellor or something."

"A what?!"

"I said don't bite my head off, I'm worried about you. I think it might help." He really was worried. He'd noticed Diana acting most unlike her, shouting at everyone, storming off every five minutes, nothing like his mild-mannered sister at all.

After many discussions between Steven, Diana their dad, and their aunt, their dad's sister Clara, it was decided that Diana would go and stay with aunt Clara for a while, which she reluctantly agreed to. She did love her aunt and she couldn't face continually seeing the hurt and confusion in her dad's face, so it wasn't too hard a decision really. Steven had spoken to his aunt and asked her if she could persuade Diana to see a counsellor. He said he would stay on to help his dad to do all the sorting out, his workplace had allowed him compassionate leave. Of course he'd discussed it with his wife, who'd had to stay in New Zealand with their children, and she had wholeheartedly agreed.

9

PRESENT DAY

Diana was a bit concerned when Louisa had rung to ask if it was okay to come home Friday afternoon until Sunday morning. "I have a day off studies on Friday mum, it will just be me. Rosie has lectures to go to."

"Is there anything wrong, darling?"

"No mum, I just fancied a break for a while."

"You and Rosie haven't had any problems, have you?"

"Nooo mum, we're all good, actually we're more than good!"

"Of course it's okay Lou Lou, you don't need to ask to come home!" Diana said, already thinking, as she spoke, that she must contact Mark and postpone the meal on Saturday, their first date! She processed that word in her thoughts. It gave her butterflies in her tummy!

After she put the phone down, Diana puzzled about Louisa's decision to come. She had a feeling there was more to it than just having a break. It would be nice for them to spend a little time together though, just the two of them, she had to admit.

Louisa made good time, considering the Friday traffic, and arrived at 12.30. She could have been earlier if she had got up a bit earlier! She guessed her mum would have prepared something for their lunch so hadn't stopped to have breakfast, which meant she was starving by the time she arrived.

"Hi mum!" she called out as she closed the door. Her mum came bustling out of the kitchen

"Oh Lou, I didn't hear you pull up! You're nice and early!" She gave her daughter a huge hug as Louisa dropped her holdall on the floor "This is such a wonderful surprise! So lovely to see you darling, come in the kitchen, I was just preparing us a bit of lunch."

"Oh good, I'm starving, I didn't stop for breakfast, it's lovely to see you too mum."

"Oh Lou! You shouldn't miss breakfast!"

"I know, I know, I wanted to get on the road."

While they were sitting with a glass of wine that evening, Louisa plucked up the courage to get to the real reason she had come and pose the question that had been preying on her mind.

"Mum? I don't want you to be upset but I sent off for my adoption certificate, as we didn't get to sort it out at Christmas, but they sent a letter to say they have no record of me having one. You've got one, though, haven't you?"

Diana had dreaded this day coming. She had been expecting it after Louisa had asked at Christmas and had now come to terms with the fact that she had to face up to it. She took a big gulp of her wine.

"I won't be a minute Lou, I have something for you."

When Diana came back into the room, she held a

document. "I should have given you this a long while ago darling, but as the years went on I could never find the right time."

"Is it my adoption certificate?"

"No darling, you were told correctly, you haven't got an adoption certificate, this is your birth certificate."

Louisa looked confused. "I don't understand, mum."

Diana handed her the document. "Read it and you'll understand."

Louisa opened it up and frowned as she read it and looked up, puzzled. "It says mother's name is you, mum."

"Oh darling Lou." Diana reached out for Louisa's hand. "This is so difficult, I need to tell you such a lot and I know I should have done so before now." She lowered her voice to barely a whisper. "It says that because I actually am your mum."

Louisa's faced clouded with anger, she snatched her hand away from Diana's. "I don't understand mum, if you're my mum why have you told me all these years, AND let everyone else believe, that you adopted me?" she said, her voice getting louder.

"There were reasons, I—"

"—You've lied to me all these years, you let me believe my birth parents didn't want me, you let me deal with the stigma of being adopted," she was shouting now. "You made up that story telling me I was 'chosen' – all fucking lies!!" Tears were running down her cheeks, her voice breaking into sobs. Diana physically flinched when Louisa swore, she had never sworn in front of her mum before. "Why? What fucking reasons could there have been to let me live a lie all my life?"

Diana flinched again. "I know it's unforgivable."

"Ya think?!!!"

"Please let me explain, Lou Lou."

"I can't take any more of this now!" Louisa said and stormed from the room, clutching her birth certificate and slamming the door so hard that a vase fell off of the shelf next to it and smashed into pieces.

Diana, already crying, looked at the broken vase, a treasured vase that her mum had loved, buried her face in her hands and sobbed. Eventually she stopped sobbing, slowly got up, got the dustpan and brush and with tears still streaming down her face she collected up all the glass, then got the vacuum cleaner out to pick up any tiny pieces. "I'm sorry, mum," she whispered.

In her bedroom, Louisa had also been sobbing, she felt totally confused and betrayed. When she had finally calmed down a little, she studied the birth certificate and it was then that she realised that under the column for Father was written *Unknown*.

Anger rose within her again, she felt that she no longer knew her mother.

Diana tapped on Louisa's door. "Please Lou, will you just let me try to explain?"

"I think you have a lot to explain, mum!" Diana slowly opened the door and as she sat on the chair next to the bed, before she had a chance to speak, Louisa said, "For a start you can tell me why my father is unknown. Did you sleep around that much?"

"NO, I did not! Louisa, how dare you think that!"

Louisa was a little taken aback at her mum's tone. "Well, why don't you know who he is?"

"I can't tell you all those details yet, darling," Diana's voice had returned to normal.

"But—" Louisa started.

Diana stopped her. "—Can I just explain that when you were born I was at my aunt's, aunty Clara in Wales, I was already seeing a counsellor because of the trauma of my mum dying so quickly and I needed it even more after the shock discovery of finding out that I was pregnant. It was a very difficult time for everyone, especially your granddad. Aunty Clara took care of me, I should have been comforting granddad, my dad, while he grieved, but I was too wrapped up in my own problems. I shall never stop feeling guilty for that."

Louisa let her mother go on, she was calming down and the emotion in her mum's voice diffused her anger a little. "Before he went back to New Zealand your uncle Steven, granddad and aunty Clara all discussed between them and decided that I should put my baby up for adoption. I needed to catch up at university, they said. But as soon as you were born I just fell in love with you, so much so that there was no way I was going to let you be adopted."

Diana tentatively took hold of Diana's hand. "I love you so much, Lou!"

Louisa left her hand in her mum's but petulantly asked, "But why the story of me being adopted, mum? Why not just tell the truth?"

"Oh darling, it was such a complicated time, it seems a bit ridiculous now, looking back. I stayed with my aunt until you were nearly two years old, I didn't go to university at all, as by then I'd decided I wanted to be a counsellor and I could study for that at evening classes. Aunty Clara helped me out a lot and I must tell you that you were so loved by everyone!"

Louisa said nothing and let her mother continue. "By then granddad was in a much better place. He's a very stoical man but it had been a lot for him to deal with, losing your gran, his beloved daughter pregnant, but once he was in a better place emotionally, I went back home. Of course I had seen him during that time, we would meet halfway. Needless to say, when I did return home, I had a beautiful little toddler with me. It just seemed so much easier on everyone around me for granddad and I to make up the story of me meeting someone and us starting the adoption process etc., the story I'd always told you, which I know now sounds silly. When you were little I couldn't tell you the truth because you wouldn't have understood and as you got older, you seemed to be quite happy about it, I didn't realise you thought there was a stigma surrounding adoption darling! And to my shame I just couldn't face telling you the truth, although I ached to let the world know you were all mine! I am so, so sorry sweetheart, I have always tried to protect you from everything and yet I've hurt you so much. I hope one day you can forgive me."

While her mother was speaking, Louisa's mood calmed even more. 'Don't judge without knowing the story,' she reminded herself. "But what about my father, mum? Did you really not know who he was?"

"Yes I did, I do, but I really can't speak about it right now, Lou. Something happened while I was in Sri Lanka which I have never spoken about to a soul. Even my mum and dad didn't know who your dad was, is. After all these years I must make contact with someone before I can say anything, which I promise I will do, but please don't ask me any more now."

"Can I just ask one more thing, mum? If it came as a shock to you that you were pregnant, does my dad know about me?"

"No darling, he doesn't."

Just then, Louisa's phone rang. "Oh, it's Rosie, mum. I need to speak to her."

"Yes, of course. I think I'm going to get ready for bed now anyway. See you in the morning." Diana kissed the top of Louisa's head and left her to speak to Rosie.

Louisa told Rosie all that had passed between her and her mum during the evening. "Christ that must have been a shock!" she said, but after Louisa had told her all the reasons why and what her mum and granddad had gone through, she added, "The thing is Lou Lou your mum could have just turned her back on you. She didn't, she gave up university so that she could keep you and it can't have been easy for her and your granddad to live apart like that. Like you, it does seem a bit odd to me that she didn't just fess up to having you and face it out, but I guess they were different times."

Diana had a very restless night. She woke once in a pool of perspiration after dreaming that her and Louisa were in Sri Lanka and a strange man was trying to pull a screaming Louisa away from her. It brought on a panic attack, she controlled her breathing and went downstairs for a glass of water.

They had a late breakfast Saturday morning as neither of them had slept well and had both slept late because of it.

"Darling, I know you have lots of questions to ask and you deserve answers. I'm so sorry I can't give them right now."

"It's okay, mum. I had a good chat with Rosie last night, she helped me get things in perspective. I'm sorry I shouted at you but it was a shock and I was in a state."

"I know, I know! I so deeply regret not telling you before, especially putting you through feeling there was a stigma towards you!"

"Oh mum, at that moment I was just trying to say things to make you feel bad, there could just as easily have been one if I had been told I was illegitimate couldn't there?"

Diana shrugged. "I guess so."

"I get now why you were so adamant about me not having a gap year and going travelling, mum."

"Yes, but it was wrong of me. I should have trusted you, not punished you for my mistakes!"

They chatted a bit more but then, after Diana asked Louisa if she would trust her to tell her about her father when she was able to, they agreed that, until Diana had sorted out the problem surrounding giving her the name of her father, they would leave it for now and just try and enjoy this rare day they had together. They went into town, did some browsing in the boutiques, had coffee, came home and had lunch, had a lazy afternoon and spent the evening watching a movie, eating chocolates and popcorn, something they hadn't done for a long time. Diana cherished these precious moments, albeit that they were brought about by something that she had put off dealing with and now had to.

Louisa left on Sunday morning after they had eaten a late breakfast. Diana gave her a huge hug before she got in the car. "I love you!" she whispered.

"I love you too, mum."

"Ring me when you get there, drive carefully!"

Afterwards, Diana made herself another coffee, sighed deeply and sat at her computer. She sighed again and started searching online. She didn't even know if he still lived in the same place after all these years. It didn't appear that he did, she would have to search further. It wasn't easy as names were all very similar. She kept reaching dead ends, she had a headache! Eventually she thought she'd give it a rest for a while.

Her phone rang. "Did you have a nice time with your daughter?"

"Oh Mark, I'm so sorry about cancelling last night. Yes and no actually."

"Do you want to talk about it?"

"Errm, not at the moment, I could do with clearing my head."

"Do you fancy a walk?"

"Actually, that would be nice."

For a while they strolled in amiable silence along the path which ran parallel with the river. Grateful to have Mark's company, Diana found the tranquility and slow lap of the water as it hit the bank calming. "Thank you for this, Mark," she said as they stopped to watch a swan serenely glide towards a patch of reeds. "It was just what I needed."

"No thanks needed, you sounded a bit down on the phone. You said yes and no: what was the no?"

Although she felt a draw to Mark, Diana wasn't ready to divulge her innermost secrets to him, especially as they hadn't even had a date yet. "Oh, nothing really wrong. I had a bit of a contretemps with Louisa about something, we sorted it out but it unsettled me and in truth I miss her when she goes back. It's nice to have a bit of company, actually."

"Sunday afternoons are not the most joyous when you're on your own. It's good to have someone to chat with on a nice walk."

Diana appreciated that he just took it for what it was, just a walk and a chat with a friend. "Oh damn! I've left my phone at home, I'm expecting Louisa to ring soon to let me know she's there. Sorry, I'll have to go back now."

"Do you think we can make a date to have another go at having that meal together?" he asked as they walked.

Having cleared her head and enjoyed Mark's company, when she got back home and checked her phone to find nothing from Louisa, Diana tried again to find the name she was looking for. Finally she found a website that claimed, as long as you had a name and a phone number, it could find any person you were looking for. She took a chance and put in his name and the only phone number she knew. She couldn't believe her luck that he must still have the same number and when it gave an address! There was no email address of course, and she didn't want to ring. She needed to get her thoughts in order and it was much easier to put it down on paper.

She started typing the letter several times, only to delete what she typed. Eventually, she settled on:

Hello Suresh,

My name is Diana. I was the au pair who looked after your sister Hiruni's two children when they were small, you may remember. You may also remember the night in the hotel before I left to come back to my sick mother. I don't think I will ever be able to forget it, or the drastic, lasting effect it has had on my life.

With the exception of the counsellor that I needed after the subsequent death of my mother, I have never told anyone of that which took place on that night. My father was dealing with my mother's illness and subsequent death and I had no wish to add to his concerns. I trust that you did as promised and dealt with the matter as it should have been dealt with?

The reason for me now writing to you is that, as a result of that night, I have a beautiful daughter. Don't worry, I am not writing for any monetary support. The reason I am writing is for the sake of my daughter. Because her birth certificate states 'Father unknown' she is now, at 18 years old, naturally curious to know who he is.

I have never divulged it to her but, as she is now speaking of DNA tests and investigations, I think the time is right for me to clarify matters for her, to save her any complications. However, I do not wish to just give her the name.

I am well aware that you would have no knowledge of her of course, but I feel the time is now right to discuss certain matters before she is made aware of who her father is. I do not want her to know everything about that night and will ensure that she never does, only for her to know who her father is.

Her name is Louisa. I have enclosed photos of her as a baby and as the beautiful woman she has become. I love her beyond measure.

I await your comments on this matter.

With regards,

Diana

She read it through several times and once satisfied put it, together with the photos, in the addressed envelope to send first thing Monday morning by recorded delivery.

She felt exhausted, she checked her phone again, nothing. She flopped back against the cushions on the sofa, going over in her mind all that had happened in the last couple of days, her eyes gradually closed and she drifted off to sleep.

She was dreaming, Suresh was banging on the door of her room in the hotel, she was crying, he kept banging the door calling her "Diana, Diana!"

She woke with a start, tears and perspiration running down her face and realised someone was banging on her front door, calling her. She grabbed a tissue, wiped her face and shakily got to the door.

"Belinda! What's wrong?"

"Are you okay Di? Louisa has been ringing you and was worried because she got no reply. She found my number in those you'd insisted she had in her phone and asked me to come and check on you."

"Come in, Bell. I don't understand, I've been waiting for her to call and checking my phone to see if she'd rung to let me know she's got there." Diana picked up her phone and sure enough there were missed calls from Louisa and a text message. She had obviously rung while Diana had been asleep, but she would have still heard the phone.

"I don't understand that!"

"You haven't got it on mute have you, Di?"

"No, I wouldn't do that, I've been waiting for her to call. Oh! Yes it is! Well, I don't know how that happened! Oh shit! She must be worried. Got time for a coffee, Bell?"

Belinda nodded as Diana scrolled through her phone. "I'll put it on and send her a text. Oh, thank you so much for coming round!"

While Diana busied herself with sorting out the coffee, Belinda followed her around, chatting. "Are you okay, Di? You looked a bit ruffled when you came to the door."

"Oh, I'd just dozed off and had a bad dream, that's all."

"Dozed off? That's not like you. Are you sure you're okay? Not feeling under the weather, are you?"

"Actually, I've had a couple of restless nights. Lou and I had a disagreement and, although we sorted it, I've felt unsettled ever since."

Belinda felt there was more to it than that. "Anything you'd like to talk about, lovely?"

Suddenly Diana felt the need to offload the burden that she'd carried with her for all these years to someone that wasn't a counsellor, the only person she had so far confided in. She knew she could trust Belinda with any secret, however dark it was.

Louisa was relieved to get her mum's text. She'd been really getting worried, especially after the strange weekend they'd had. She was glad she had Rosie to confide in. She didn't have that sort of close relationship with Katy and Emily. Well, of course, not as close as her and Rosie had!

"So is your mum going to tell you about your dad?"

"I hope so, but God knows what the big secret is. She refused to speak about it until she'd made contact with someone."

"What – your dad?"

"I guess so, she was very closed up about it. To be honest, Rosie, after I'd calmed down a bit I felt a bit sorry for her as something obviously happened to her while she was in Sri Lanka. I didn't even realise that my gran died so soon after mum got home from there."

"So have you forgiven her for telling you all these years that you were adopted?"

"Not entirely. Although I *think* I understand, it's certainly changed things a bit between us."

Rosie pulled her into a cuddle.

10

Mark picked Diana up at 8pm on Wednesday. She was looking forward to having an evening out. She'd been under such a strain and her relationship with Louisa was rather fragile at the moment. She had asked Diana if she had contacted the person and was impatient for a reply. It didn't matter how many times Diana said she would let her know when she had any news!

"You look very nice!" Mark said when she opened the door.

"Well thank you, kind sir!" she said with a little curtsy.

He laughed. "Your chariot awaits, m'lady!" He tugged his imaginary forelock, they both chuckled.

The restaurant was pretty full and quite noisy, their table was right in the middle so it was difficult to have a decent conversation. Diana said she would rather skip a starter and just have main and dessert.

Mark agreed. He said when they'd eaten, "It's a bit noisy tonight, would you rather skip coffee?"

"Oh I was hoping you would say that!" Diana said with relief.

When they were back in the car, Mark asked, "Would you like to go anywhere else?"

"No thank you Mark, the meal was lovely, thank you, it was just a shame it was so noisy and we missed our coffee. Would you like to have coffee at mine?" She hoped she wasn't giving him the wrong signals by suggesting that!

"How do you like your coffee, Mark?" she shouted from the kitchen.

"Oh, strong and black please!"

They chatted easily with each other. Mark took her hand. "I've really enjoyed this evening."

She left his hand there. "So have I, I enjoy your company." He leaned in closer. Diana thought, 'Oh God, he's going to kiss me!' It surprised her to realise that she wanted him to. It wasn't a passionate kiss – not at first, but it became passionate. He kissed her neck, she tingled and gave an involuntary moan and tilted her head back, his mouth moved down to her throat as he undid her blouse, she felt the anticipation... and then the flashbacks came, as they always did. She pulled away, breathless, her breathing became difficult, she did her breathing exercises.

"I'm... s sorry, so... sorry," she said between short breaths.

Mark was alarmed. "What is it? What's wrong? Did I do something? I'm sorry, did I read it wrong? Should I have taken things slower? Are you okay?" He fired the questions at her so quickly.

When Diana had her breathing more in control, she took Mark's hand. "No, you did nothing wrong, you read it right, I wanted what was going to happen. It's me, Mark," she said, as tears rolled down her cheeks.

He held her hand tightly. "Can you talk about it?"

For the first time, when she got to this point with a man, she felt that she could and slowly, between fits of sobbing, she told Mark her story, he gripping her hands and comforting her as she did so.

When she had finally come to the end, he took her in his arms. "My poor darling. It's okay, we can take things as slowly as you like. We can do things at a pace you're comfortable with. I will help you through this. I like you a lot, Di."

Diana lifted her tear-stained face. "Do you mean that? You're not put off with that story?"

"Yes, of course I mean it, I'm a very stubborn fella, ya know!" he said with a grin.

She kissed him hard on the mouth. "Thank you, I like a stubborn fella," she added with a small smile.

Later that evening, when she was on her own, she felt a certainty that this man was going to be with her for at least a lot longer than any previous one. She didn't dare hope that it would be for good, but she had a good feeling and a faint hope that he really might help her to face her demons.

11

Diana was surprised, not only to have received a reply to her letter, but that it took nowhere near as long as she thought it might. Her hand shook as she opened it, unsure of what kind of reply it would be. She read it quickly, then read it again more slowly, absorbing every word. It was not the response she had expected, although she actually didn't know what she had expected. The news in it came as a shock and she knew that it wasn't going to be what Louisa wanted to hear, either. She wondered if there was a possibility that Louisa could get home again for a weekend. She didn't like her driving on that long journey but didn't want to tell her the contents of the letter over the phone. They both knew there was a compromise in buying this house but had agreed that Diana needed to be able to have a reasonable daily commute to her consulting rooms so had moved from the south side of the town to the north, saving Louisa about half an hour on her journey and only adding half an hour to Diana's.

She rang Louisa that evening. "I've received a reply."

"Oh great! What does it say?"

"Well, I don't really want to talk about it over the phone, Lou. Is there a chance that you could get home this weekend? I don't like to ask you to make that journey, or what about if I came to you? I could do that, I just thought we'd be more comfortable chatting here."

"Mum, listen a minute!"

Diana realised that she hadn't come up for breath or let Louisa get a word in! "Sorry darling, I'm listening."

"I don't mind making the journey, I—"

"—I'll help you with the petrol money, of course."

"MUM!"

"Sorry, carry on."

"I was going to say my last course finishes early Friday so I can leave straight after and get home before dark."

"Oh that's brilliant, darling! Will Rosie be coming with you? Only so that I know what to prepare."

"I'm not sure what her study diary is, mum, but I'll text you when we've sorted it out so you'll know."

Diana was really enjoying the life-coach course, and not just because Mark was there. She was already getting ready some templates for different aspects of her business portfolio and planned to scale down the counselling side. All this, of course, in between coping with the other dramas in her life.

She was telling Belinda all this when they met up for a coffee one lunchtime.

"I'm really pleased for you, Di. I know you'll be brilliant at it, you have the right personality. So what time is Louisa due tomorrow?"

"They should be here between 6 and 6.30," she said.

"Oh, is Rosie coming after all, then?"

"Yes, I think Lou is pleased she can. I think she needs her support. It's a huge thing going on in her life, isn't it?"

"It really is, but she seems quite a strong girl, your Louisa."

She heard the car pull up just as she was putting the finishing touches to the table. She went down to the car to greet them, giving them both big hugs. "Did you have a good journey?"

"Well, we did catch some of the rush-hour traffic but it wasn't too bad, was it?" Louisa said, turning to Rosie.

"No, not bad at all."

Diana ushered them into the house. "Take your things up. I've put you both in the twin room, is that okay?"

"It's fine, mum." Louisa was amazed at how free-thinking her mum was, as she probably knew full well what might happen between them and had given them the bedroom which would give them that freedom. Although she was still coming to terms with her mum's big lie, at this moment she really loved her!

"Dinner will be ready in about 20 minutes!" Diana shouted after them.

But Louisa didn't want to wait until after dinner to know the contents of the letter. "Well, mum? What did it say? Why couldn't you tell me on the phone?"

"Oh Lou, the dinner will spoil!"

"Mum! Just tell me!!"

"Well, sit down then. Come round here, Rosie, so you can sit next to her. I didn't want to tell you over the phone because it's a bit upsetting. Your father is not a well man, in fact he is very ill. However, when he heard about you and because he is very ill he has asked if he could meet you. It was a shock to him to find out that he has a daughter, of course."

Louisa was gripping Rosie's hand. "So do you think he would have wanted to meet me if he wasn't very ill?"

"Oh darling I don't know, but it doesn't really matter does it?"

Louisa had tears in her eyes. "But we don't break up from uni for another three weeks, mum. Supposing he... you know? Oh! Does that mean we have to go to Sri Lanka?!! Can we afford to go?"

Diana put her hand on Louisa's arm. "I don't know the answers to all these questions at the moment, darling. I have an email address now so I can make contact with the person who gave me this information and see what they say, but I wanted to tell you what the letter said first."

"Can I see the letter, mum?"

"Would you mind if I kept it for now, Lou? There are things written in it that are personal to me, but I will show you when the time is right. Is that okay?"

Louisa didn't really like this secretiveness and was ready to have another outburst but Rosie, sensing this, squeezed her hand and gave a little, almost imperceptive, shake of her head. "Yes, I suppose so, mum."

"Look, can we just eat now girls?"

"Oh mum, I couldn't eat anything!"

"You have to eat something, Lou! And besides I've not prepared it all for it to go to waste!" Diana felt guilty for snapping, knowing this was all very traumatic for Louisa, but it was traumatic for her too, emotions were running high. "Look darling, once we've eaten perhaps you girls could clear away while I get some things sorted out. How does that sound?" Diana needed time to think, she had started forming a plan in her mind and decided that after the weekend she would put it in place.

Diana took the ring from the box in the back of the drawer of her dressing table with shaking hands. She had been tempted many times to sell it and had always resisted, but she felt that, because of the reason, now was the right time. She took it to a jeweller in the high street, a very reputable company.

Diana had always determined that she would ensure Louisa would get to university, no matter what the hardship was and although the rest of her small inheritance from her gran had helped, it did mean finances were often stretched, so flights to, and hotel accommodation in Sri Lanka were not really within the realms of her financial capabilities.

She was shocked at the value the jeweller put on the ring! And he was willing to buy it! She went back the following day, after giving it more thought and making her decision. Then she went straight back home to go online and book everything. She had re-scheduled clients, which she hated doing as it upset the fluidity of their sessions, but these were special circumstances. She rang Louisa.

"Hi darling, it's all sorted. We leave Saturday evening on the night flight."

"Oh wow, really mum? How did you manage that?"

"Never mind how, Lou, it's all sorted and as the university has confirmed your leave of absence, when you get home Friday evening we'll get packed!"

"Ooh I can't believe I'm going to meet my dad AND I'm going to Sri Lanka!" Louisa was beside herself with excitement.

Diana, on the other hand, was actually really dreading it. She wasn't totally sure she would be able to deal with seeing him again, even being in the same country again. She made an appointment to see her counsellor. He was fully booked but, when she told him what was happening, he gave her an emergency appointment for Thursday evening. Diana knew that he couldn't do anything to change how she would feel, she just wanted to tell someone how she felt and why and he was the only person she could tell all to.

12

"**G**od mum, it's hot isn't it?" Diana was transported in time back to the day she arrived, when it was the heat that had hit her, too.

"Are you okay, mum?"

"Oh yes darling. Sorry, I was miles away. Yes it is a bit warm, isn't it?"

Diana went through all of the customs procedures and baggage claim in a daze. She kept having flashbacks of memory, even imagined she saw the little smiling man holding up the board with her name on it.

"Oh is that our taxi man, mum?"

Diana jolted and realised it wasn't her imagination, though it wasn't the same man of course, that was just in her memory. "Errm yes it is, make sure you've got everything Lou."

Diana had booked a different hotel on the other side of town this time. She didn't think she could cope with being in the same one as before. It meant a longer taxi ride but she felt it was worth it. She'd booked them a twin room.

"Oh this is lovely, mum!"

'Bless you,' Diana thought. 'This is such a big adventure for you, you cannot know what an ordeal it is for me!'

After breakfast the next morning, Diana ordered a taxi. "Right Lou, let's go and get our bits and pieces ready and wait back down here in the foyer." Diana couldn't stop shaking, she hadn't eaten much of her breakfast and her stomach was churning. It took all her self control and breathing exercises to prevent a panic attack!

When they were in the taxi Diana's heart was racing and the nearer they got to where they were meeting, the more it raced! When they arrived, she saw him immediately. She recognised him even after all the years that had passed.

"Who's that, mum? He's very handsome!"

"He is going to take us to the nursing home."

"To see my father?"

"Yes darling." Diana could see that Louisa was almost bursting with emotion.

"Hello Diana, you look very well and this must be Louisa?"

"Hello Suresh, yes, this is Louisa."

"I'm very pleased to meet you, you are even more beautiful than your photo!"

Louisa coyly shook his proffered hand and shyly said, "Thank you, pleased to meet you."

"I appreciate you setting up this meeting, Suresh, it means a lot to Louisa."

"It is my pleasure, although that probably isn't a good choice of words." He looked a little embarrassed.

"Can we go now?" Diana asked, not wanting to prolong this waiting time any longer.

"Yes of course, my car is just over there." He motioned to the young man standing by the car, who instantly came and ushered them towards the vehicle.

"How are Ashan and Eshani, Suresh? They must be adults and probably married by now."

"They are very well, yes, Ashan is now 25 years old and is an accountant in a large company, he has recently become engaged to be married. Eshani is now 28 years old. She has her own company."

"That doesn't surprise me!" Diana said with a smile.

On the journey, Louisa couldn't contain herself any longer. "Is my father looking forward to seeing me?"

"Yes, he is."

"What's wrong with him? Why is he so ill?"

"Louisa!" Diana snapped.

"It's fine, Diana, the young lady has a right to know. He has terminal pancreatic cancer, Louisa. He has been ill for some time and is now in palliative care, which means his life expectancy is now quite limited."

Suresh led the way when they got to the nursing home. "This way, he is in this room." Suresh opened the door.

Diana wasn't prepared for what she saw. This man was but a shadow of the man she last remembered. She felt hot, she shook, she had a rushing in her ears, his face faded and she sank to the floor.

13

She was back in that hotel room. Ravan had brought her bags up for her and asked her if she was okay. Suddenly all her emotions erupted. She was so worried about her mum, the sudden and abrupt way in which she had to leave, the feeling of being far away from home, feeling very scared, it all just poured from her in gulps and sobs, she couldn't stop it, his kind words had opened flood gates. He put his arms around her and held her tight. "It's okay, it has been a shock, you will be fine," he said soothingly.

Gradually, her sobs subsided. She realised she was in his arms. It felt wrong, she pulled away. "I'm sorry!" she said weakly.

"Everything is okay, Diana. You don't have to worry," he said, pulling her back towards him.

"No, please, I'm okay now, I—"

"—I said you don't have to worry, it will be alright, just relax."

"No, stop – please!" she shouted.

He put his hand over her mouth. "Please don't shout, don't

struggle, I don't want to hurt you. I won't hurt you if you just relax." She was petrified, she knew what he intended to do, she thought of her ill mum, she didn't want to not get to her, she had to be able to leave here, she was shaking, her thoughts tumbled around her head, and all the while Ravan was guiding her backwards towards the bed, 'what if he kills me?' She made a decision. She let him push her gently back onto the bed, push up her skirt and pull down her knickers. He became animated and undid his trousers, he already had an erection. She lay lifeless and had no feeling except revulsion as he entered her, silent tears streaming down her face as he climaxed and ejaculated. "Good girl!" he breathed. He slowly got to his feet, adjusting his clothing, and suddenly looked shocked and horrified. His face contorted, he muttered, "I'm so sorry!" And ran from the room.

There was a banging at the door. "Diana, Diana, it's Suresh! Please, I want to help you."

She opened the door to show him that his worst fears were right. "Oh my poor girl, did he hurt you?" She numbly shook her head. He got her a glass of water and went to hold her arm to sit her down. She flinched. "I won't hurt you, Diana."

"That's what he said," she replied.

"I'm so very sorry you have had this dreadful experience. He has a mental illness, which is controlled with drugs, but…" His voice trailed off. "That's why I'm always about. My sister should never have let him bring you here alone," he ended angrily. "I know you need to get back for your mother but I will take you to the police station to report this."

Diana looked up sharply, thoughts whirring around in her

head. She didn't like the thought of going through all this with the police now and didn't want any delays getting home.

Diana dabbed her eyes. "I don't want to do that. I cannot right now tell all that's just happened to me to the police, it's too distressing." She began to cry again. "I don't want any holdups, I must get home, I want to see my mum, I think she's very ill!"

Suresh could not hide the intensity of his anger. "I know you do, Diana. I cannot tell you how sorry I am that you have had to go through this. Are you sure he didn't hurt you in any way?"

Diana wiped her eyes once again. "No Suresh, he just raped me!" she said bitterly.

Suresh removed a ring from his finger. "Would you take this as a gesture of my goodwill for what has happened?"

"What, like a bribe?" she replied angrily.

"No, no, no, not at all, I am just trying to make up for what my brother-in-law has done and I promise you that I will ensure this will be dealt with, Diana."

14

"Diana, Diana!"

"Mum, mum! Are you okay?"

Diana regained consciousness to see Suresh and Louisa standing over her and that a nurse was patting her brow with a damp cloth. "You fainted, it sometimes happens when seeing a very sick person. You'll be okay. Here, have a drink of water."

Diana felt anything but okay, but gradually became aware of where they were and why they were here. She shakily stood up, walked towards the bed, turned to Louisa and whispered, "This is your father. I'm sorry, I need to leave." She couldn't stay there any longer and left the room.

When Diana had gone, Louisa went up to the sunken looking man in the bed. He lifted his hand, she took it, and said "Hello... father." She didn't really know how she felt, it wasn't quite the bells and whistles feeling she'd expected, yet she felt some sort of emotion. She thought perhaps it was just the knowledge of knowing there was a real person that she could pin the label of father to.

Suresh put his hand on her shoulder. "Are you okay, Louisa?"

"Yes, thank you, I'm okay. I'd better go and see if mum is alright, I know this has been difficult for her, but I didn't expect her to run off like that."

Diana had absolutely refused to tell Louisa the story of her and Ravan when she asked. How could she possibly tell her that she was the result of a rape?!! She had never told her that she was a result of a loving liaison, but she knew that's what Louisa probably guessed and she had no qualms about not disillusioning her.

"Perhaps she didn't expect to be so affected by her memories," was all Suresh said. "I believe that you are here for a few days? So perhaps you can come again if you want to?"

"Yes we are, thank you."

They found Diana outside. "I'm sorry I had to rush off like that but I just found it all too much," she said to both Louisa and Suresh.

"I understand," Suresh said. Louisa just asked if her mum was alright. She didn't quite know what else to say, she felt a little bit as though she was on the outside of something that everyone else was part of.

Suresh insisted on driving them back to the hotel. When they arrived, Diana asked Louisa if she could meet her up in the room. "I have some things to chat to Suresh about, Lou."

Again Louisa felt that she was being left out of some mystery but did as her mother asked and said her goodbyes to Suresh. "Thank you for taking us," she said.

"My pleasure, Louisa," he replied.

When they were alone, he turned to Diana. "She is a beautiful girl Diana, you have done a wonderful job of bringing her up on your own."

"Thank you. It was a struggle sometimes but she's worth it!"

"I am truly sorry that you had that struggle. I knew that night and what happened was traumatic for you, but I could not have had any idea that you would have had even more than that to deal with, I really am so sorry."

"I appreciate that, Suresh. I wanted to ask you about Ravan. You said at the time of the... errm on that night that he had a mental illness. You said in your letter that you had done as promised and dealt with what he did. What happened?"

"Yes, I did. As you had no wish to endure the trauma of reliving it all for the police, and I really understood why at the time, I could not report the incident to them, but I knew something had to be done. I forced my sister to come to terms with the fact that the problem was drastic and that it had to be dealt with urgently, so he was admitted to a special clinic, after being re-assessed, following a confidential statement that I made. Unfortunately, Hiruni couldn't deal with it all and they later divorced. When he finally came out of the clinic, he became a recluse."

Despite herself and what he'd put her through, Diana felt some empathy for the man. In her role as counsellor, she came across many troubled souls. She could never forgive him for the emotional harm he had subsequently done to her but she no longer felt bitter and angry.

"What was his reaction when you told him of Louisa's existence?"

"He was of course shocked initially but once the news had sunk in, he was actually very pleased."

"Do Eshani and Ashan know that they have a half-sister?"

"Yes, I told them. They would like to meet her if Louisa would like that."

"Thank you for your kindness in all this Suresh and I have never thanked you for coming back to the hotel that night to make sure I was okay, so thank you."

"It is I who must thank you, Diana. It was an unacceptable thing I asked of you."

15

Diana and Louisa went back to the nursing home twice during their stay. Each time Diana waited outside for Louisa, much to Louisa's puzzlement, but she respected her mother's wishes. She still didn't quite know what she felt about Ravan. She knew that, even if he hadn't been dying, she would probably not have had a close relationship with him, especially as he lived so far away, but she was happy that she did, at least, have a father that she had met. She said all this to Rosie when they were having one of their many chats.

They also met up with her half-siblings. They both remembered Diana, though Ashan's memory was not as sharp as Eshani's. He had been only six years old, after all! It shook both Diana and Louisa to see how much she looked like Eshani! Louisa found it all rather strange, after being an only child for so long, to suddenly find that she had half-siblings. Louisa guessed that the reason her mother was adamant about not telling her the story was because she'd had an affair with a married man. Diana neither denied nor confirmed and remained tight-lipped. Diana showed Louisa a bit of the area while they were there, she was fascinated! Suresh insisted on collecting them the morning of their departure to take them to the airport.

It was a much different departure this time.

She had relived time and again that last evening. After Suresh had left her, she had stood in the shower sobbing and scrubbing herself so hard her body was bright red. She couldn't get the image of Ravan's wild-eyed, shocked look out of her head, kept hearing him say 'good girl'. She eventually got out of the shower, her skin was so sore she patted herself dry. She went to bed but slept fitfully, with lurid dreams. She made the journey to the airport and the flight home in a complete daze.

Everyone at home attributed the way she looked, her moods, her general dispirited manner to her shock at seeing how ill her mum was, and of course that was a huge part of it but, it was just an additional reason and Diana didn't tell a soul. Looking back she was pleased that the decision had been made for her to stay with her aunt once it was evident that she was pregnant. It was easier in some ways on her dad and certainly helped her to get through the pregnancy, looking after Louisa and studying as well. She was so grateful to all of them for not pushing her to tell them the circumstances of her becoming pregnant. She just said, "I made a mistake, I'm so sorry dad!"

Diana had some money left from the sale of the ring (she still couldn't get over the amount of money she'd received for it) and decided to use it to invest in a larger practice to rent. She'd found one not too far from her current practice and intended to combine the counselling and life-coach service. Since her return from Sri Lanka, her and Mark had become much closer and after much debate had decided to go into partnership for the life-coaching side of the practice, so that Diana could still concentrate mainly on the counselling.

True to his word, Mark didn't rush her into having sex. They petted and fondled but he never pushed to take it further. Something had changed in Diana since seeing Ravan in the hospital bed, though. Whenever her and Mark got near to taking it further, it wasn't Ravan's wild-eyed face that came into her head, it was the image of a sick man, and gradually she was able to bat the image away.

Mark had cooked her a surprise meal, the table was decorated nicely and he opened a nice bottle of wine. "That was delicious! You kept that a secret, that you're such a good cook! Thank you for this evening." Diana looked up into his eyes as he poured her another glass of wine, she lifted her mouth to his, he lifted her up from the chair saying, "The pleasure is all mine," and kissed her passionately. She responded eagerly, he nibbled her ear and whispered, "Would you like to go upstairs?" She kissed him again and pulled him towards the stairs. They stumbled up the stairs, undressing as they went. They fell onto the bed, he kissed her neck, lowered his kisses to her breasts, she writhed beneath him, he stopped, looked into her eyes and whispered, "Are you sure?"

"Yes – I am," and for the first time since Ravan had raped her Diana was able to enjoy full, passionate, fulfilling, wonderful sex with a man she now knew she loved.

16

It was a busy year when Diana and Mark got married – after which Mark officially adopted Louisa, which delighted her; Belinda and Paul's daughter Saffy married Tom; and Louisa and Rosie got engaged.

Ravan, who had died three weeks after their visit, had left Louisa some money in his will, with the stipulation that she should use it once she graduated to help her in her career as a doctor. She had told him her aspirations when chatting on one of her visits to him. When Louisa and Rosie *did* both graduate, Diana and Mark held a big party, inviting Belinda, Paul, their girls and their partners, Rosie's uncle and his wife and Mark's sister and brother-in-law.

When the party was in full swing, Diana sent Louisa to see who was at the door. She squealed with pleasure when she opened it. "It's Suresh!" They had kept in contact with Suresh after their visit and she looked upon him as an honorary uncle. "Oh mum, did you do this?"

"Well, Mark and I implemented it but, of course, Suresh had to make the journey."

Louisa hugged him. "Thank you for coming!" He was her link to her origins.

For Diana, this signalled the start of something good that was to come out of the awful experience that had dogged her life until recent times. She felt more positive about life than she ever had. She could even now look at Suresh without reliving those awful memories, and Louisa's happiness was enough to outshine anything! There were already talks between Louisa, Rosie and Suresh of future holidays in Sri Lanka! Although Louisa wouldn't have the relationship she'd hoped for with the father she had so wanted to know, she now had a connection with him through Suresh.

My thanks go to my two wonderful daughters, my family and the dear friends who believed in and encouraged me in this venture and a huge thanks to Claire Wingfield, without whom this book would never have come to fruition.

If you've enjoyed reading, please take the time to leave a short review on Amazon or elsewhere online. These are a huge help to authors.